Be[illegible]

Immortality

Book 3

A Thunder of Dragons

By

Paul J. Kearns

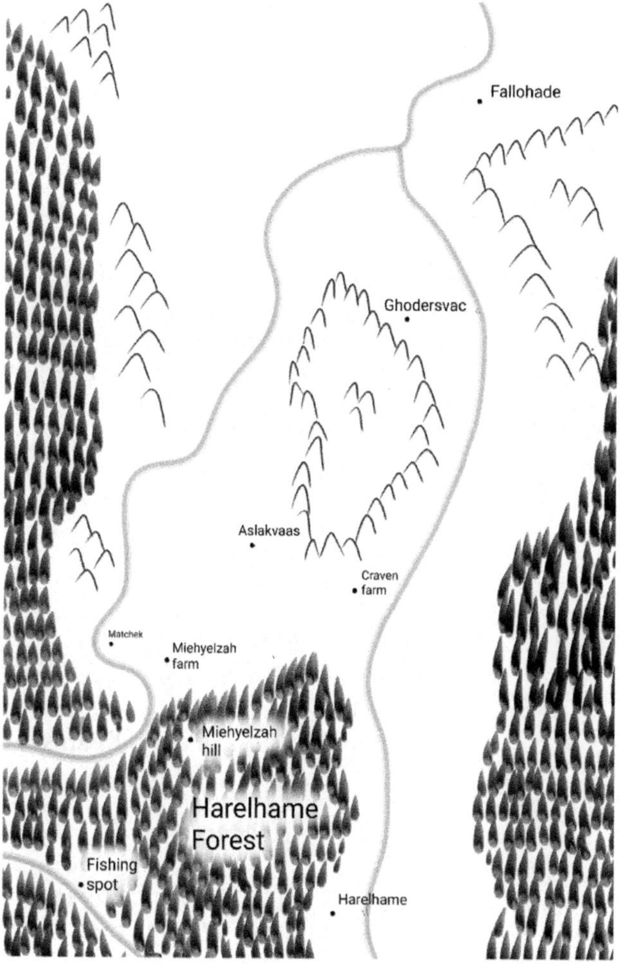
Fallohade
Ghodersvac
Aslakvaas
Craven
farm
Matchek
Miehyelzah
farm
Miehyelzah
hill
Harelhame
Forest
Fishing
spot
Harelhame

Paperback ISBN: 9781739784423
Ebook ISBN: 9781739784430

For Carrie, Quinn, and Erin.
I love you all without end.

For Phil, Karis, Chris, Dany, Andy, Bryan, and all of you who have followed and supported me through this process. It has been a long time, but we are finally here.

Thank you so much.

This book is a work of fiction. All names, characters, locations, and incidents are either a product of the author's imagination or are used fictitiously. Any resemblance to actual events, locations, or persons, living, dead or undead, or immortal is entirely coincidental.

Paul J. Kearns asserts the moral right to be identified as the as the author of this work.

Content Warning:
Death, animal death, injury detail, graphic gore, torture, blood drinking, dismemberment, mutilation,

Acknowledgements:

Thank you to Carrie, Quinn, and Erin for all your love and support.
Thank you to my Mum, Dad, for bringing me up right, for teaching me that I can shape my own future and teaching me to go and get what I want from life.
Thank you to Noel and Sam for the ongoing support and for believing in me.
Thank you to Louise Croft for all your help.
Thank you to all my extended family for being there when we have needed you most and for being amazing.
Thank you to all my friends, you know who you are and know I love you.
To Mr. Roberts, my former English teacher at Little lever secondary school as it was back then, thank you for being a great teacher and encouraging me to continue writing fiction.

www.pauljkearns.com

PJKauthor@hotmail.com

Other books by Paul J. Kearns:

The Hunted and other Twisted Tales.

Special Operations vampire Elimination Unit

Beasts of Immortality book 1: Blood and Purpose

Beasts of Immortality book 2: Armed to the Teeth

We, The Damned

You can find Paul J. Kearns on social media.

https://m.facebook.com/PJKearnsAuthor/

www.instagram.com/pauljkearnsauthor/

linktr.ee/PaulJKearns

tinyurl.com/PJKamazon

TikTok handle: @pauljkearns_author

Chapter 1.

Roughly 5000 years ago, on the land mass that would come to be known as northern Europe.

Anzo Miehyelzah and his son Ruhsarr walked through the forest that ran along the borders of their farmland. Anzo swept the ground with his eyes until he saw what he was looking for. He put his hand out to stop Ruhsarr and they crouched down next to the animal tracks.

"You see this?" said Anzo.

"Yes, is that him?" said Ruhsarr.

"It looks around the same size as the tracks in our land, and this would be his territory. So yeah, I'd say it's him," he said.

He stood and looked around at the surrounding trees. His eyes searched for and followed the tracks that the animal had left. There were broken branches ahead in the trees where it had pushed its way through the undergrowth

"Looks like he went this way," said Anzo.

They followed the tracks for another mile until they reached a small hill and an area of raised craggy ground beyond it.

"Get down, son," whispered Anzo. "He's just over the hill."

They both got down onto the forest floor.

"How can you tell?" whispered Ruhsarr.

"Come on, son, use your senses," whispered Anzo.

Ruhsarr listened but heard nothing. He sniffed the air. The smell of wet grass rushed into his nostrils.

"I smell him," whispered Ruhsarr.

"Yes, you do," whispered Anzo.

They crawled to the crest of the hill and looked

over. A Huge brown bear stood scratching its back against a tree.

"Wow. He's a big lad," whispered Anzo.

"What are we going to do?" whispered Ruhsarr. He felt the hair stand up on his neck.

"He's upwind from us, so right now he doesn't know we're here. When we move in on him, he will be aggressive so we need to attack before he can attack us. You can't show any fear. You need to be fierce and fast. The first strikes need to be as deadly as possible or he will kill us," whispered Anzo.

"Could we just hunt something else?" whispered Ruhsarr with a frown.

"I wish we could, son, but we need his meat and fur. He will feed and clothe us for a whole moon," whispered Anzo.

"I understand," whispered Ruhsarr and nodded.

"Ready your axe. When I tap your shoulder, we run in and cut him down," whispered Anzo.

Ruhsarr nodded. They watched the bear as he fell back down onto all fours and trudged towards the mouth of his cave. Anzo raised his hand over Ruhsarr's shoulder and held it there. The younger man could feel his heart beating heavily in his chest as excitement rushed through him. He hoped his father was feeling the same. The bear stopped and rotated its head to the right. As it began to shake Anzo placed his hand down on Ruhsarr's shoulder. The two men stood and ran silently towards the beast. As they got close Anzo approached from the right and Ruhsarr approached from the left. The older man raised his axe over his head while the younger man swung the axe he had spent the previous day sharpening out to his side. As Anzo brought his axe down toward its head, the bear heard Ruhsarr's foot falls and turned its head to the left. The older man's axe crashed down into the moss-covered ground. The bear snapped its head back to the right and knocked Anzo off his feet. As he hit the ground the bear sunk its teeth into his thigh just above the knee and effortlessly swung him like a ragdoll. Anzo felt his muscles tearing and screamed. The bear slammed him down onto the ground and knocked the air out of him. It strode over to him and opened its jaws. Anzo pushed his hand against the bears head and plunged his iron dagger down, but it glanced off the bear's thick skull. It let out a pained cry as Ruhsarr buried his axe deep into the left side of its neck. As he pulled the axe free from its flesh it reared up and roared. Blood spurt from the deep wound that had sliced right through an artery. It stumbled and whined and swatted at Ruhsarr with its front right paw. The movement was weak though and it did little more than knock him away a little. It then fell down onto its side, whined once more, then its head slumped to the rocky ground, and it was still. Ruhsarr stood panting for a moment.

"Son, help me," said Anzo.

He ran over to his father and inspected his wounds. He took a small package from the wrap he wore around his waist and opened it, inside there was a small wooden bowl, a skin bladder full of water, a mixture of herbs, berries and minerals, and some strips of material and leather for binding wounds. He put the herbs, berries and minerals into a bowl and added a little water from the bladder and mixed them together into a poultice. He spread some of it on a leaf and placed it over the wound on Anzo's leg. He then bound it with a strip of material and added a strip of leather to hold it in place.

"That will help for now, but we need to take you to the healer as soon as we can," said Ruhsarr.

"Thank you, son. Thank the gods for you. Your

axe was surely guided by them today," said Anzo.

"I think it was. It was the work of a divine hand. Come, we have to get him back home," said Ruhsarr.

"First we must thank him, son," said Anzo.

The Two men knelt down beside the bear, and each placed a hand upon its fur.

"As our fathers have done before us and as our children will do when we are gone, we thank you. For your speed, your strength, your sight, your hearing, and your sense of smell. We hope you will pass these abilities onto us through the gifts of your flesh and your furs. The great circle continues, your death gives life to us and many more. May you run free in the hallowed forests of the next life," they said in unison.

"Fetch Yannee. I will stay here and defend the bear," said Anzo.

After a short walk Ruhsarr reached the small clearing where they had left the tall and strong horse, Yannee. He had his head down and was grazing on the small patch of grass there. When he heard the footsteps approaching he quickly raised his head. Seeing that it was just Ruhsarr he shook his long mane and nickered.

"Hello, boy," said Ruhsarr and ran his hand along the horse's long muscular neck. Yannee nuzzled the side of the man's head.

"Come on. Let's go and help dad," said Ruhsarr. He led and Yannee followed.

They cut down some small trees to make a sled to transport the carcass back to the farm. This was attached to the horse's harness. Anzo also fashioned a walking stick from one of the branches. With his injuries limiting his movement and having to pick a path both Yannee and the sled could navigate made the journey a slow process.

Half the day had passed when they arrived at their farm. Their home was a long rectangular building made of stones and mud with a wood and thatched roof. The first room was made for cooking and sleeping. There was a stone lined fire pit in the centre of the room, hey lined sack beds, and many animal skins for warmth. The next room was used as a stable, where they would tend to their animals, and sheer the sheep. The third room was where they stored foods and smoked the meats. Outside there was a wooden outhouse and a stone building for smelting and smithing metal

They skinned the pelt from the bear and hung it up to dry. They then removed the limbs and divided the torso. Every part of the animal would be used. The bones and teeth were saved for broth, the internal organs would be made into stews, and the digestive tract would be used for water pouches and bow strings among other things.

Some of the meat was salted and they put it into their storage building in two piles. One for them and the other to trade at the market in Aslakvaas the next day. The rest was hung in the smoking room.

Ruhsarr then helped Anzo onto the back of their horse, Yannee, and they set off to see the healer.

Chapter 2.

They skirted the edge of the forest until they approached a circle of stones. These were granite boulders ranging from waist to chest height. They had been moved here long before Anzo's father was born. A symbol was painted in blood on each stone. As they got closer Ruhsarr shuddered which caused Anzo to turn and look at him.

"This place scares me," said Ruhsarr.

"You are right to be scared. This is a place of old power. There are forces at work here that keep us safe by driving out the Shrak. To fear this place instinctively shows wisdom," said Anzo.

They passed into the stone circle and could see the roofs of nine short houses arranged in a circle. This was the little village of Matchek. As they approached smoke rose from most of the houses. Strings of bones and wooden sticks twisted and knocked together in the air causing an eerie clacking that was said to sound like the voices of the spirit world. It gave the area an otherworldly atmosphere.

"Let's just get what we need and leave," said Ruhsarr.

Anzo nodded and grunted in agreement.

A fire burned in the centre of the circle of houses. Two women and a man stood naked beside the fire with their arms raised. As they looked into the flames they swayed from side to side.

"You come seeking a remedy?" said a voice from the house closest to Anzo and Ruhsarr.

They turned to see an elderly man with long grey hair stood in the doorway.

"Yes, we do," said Anzo.

"Come closer. They call me Skalat," said the man.

They walked towards him as he stepped back into the house and waved them in. Ruhsarr helped Anzo down from the horse and supported him as he limped into the house.

"I am Anzo, and this is my son, Ruhsarr."

"Your leg ails you. What happened?" said Skalat.

"We were hunting a bear. He managed to bite my leg in the process," said Anzo.

"Sit, let me see," said Skalat

Ruhsarr helped Anzo to the ground. Anzo then removed the clothing from his leg and unfastened the strips of leather and material. Skalat looked at the wound and manipulated Anzo's leg, turning the foot left to right and bending the knee. He looked at the poultice on the leaf too.

"This poultice. It's good. What is it?" said Skalat.

"It's Elderberries, nettles, and Marigolds," said Ruhsarr.

Skalat smiled and nodded.

"It has done its work. In exchange for some of that bear meat, I have something better," said Skalat.

Ruhsarr looked down at the bundle at his hip then back to the man.

"Very well," said Ruhsarr with a nod and handed the bundle over.

Skalat reached for a pouch and poured out a mix of what looked like salt and dried fish scales into a bowl. He added a chunk of bee's wax and honey and crushed it all together. He then worked this poultice onto Anzo's wound and covered it with a clean cloth and tied it into place.

"Keep that on for three days. Do not remove it before then. Keep it clean of dirt and creepy crawlies. Then the wound will be healed. After that bury it far away. The crawlies love the honey," said Skalat

"Thank you," said Anzo.

Ruhsarr helped him to his feet, and they made to leave.

Be careful on your way home. Be inside before nightfall," said Skalat.

"Thank you again," said Anzo.

Ruhsarr looked across to the blazing fire and the chanting people and then back to the man.

"Do you not worry about the things in the night?" said Ruhsarr.

"They know better than to come here," said Skalat.

The fire then burned higher with a purple flame and he smiled.

"Well," said Ruhsarr.

"We best be on our way, said Anzo.

They both climbed onto Yannee's back and made a hasty departure.

Chapter 3.

Anzo still limped a little as they approached the town of Aslakvaas the next morning. The roads were bustling with people who were also there to trade goods. There were people here from the surrounding towns of Ghodersvac and Harelhame. Some were even from as far away as Fallohade. As they guided their horse and cart under the gateway and into the town square there was an air of frivolity and joviality. People were singing and playing instruments. While others danced and children ran around and played. Friends met each other and talked around the stalls that sold ales and breads. Anzo and Ruhsarr found an area and set up their stall on a rudimentary table. Above it was a woven cover of dried reeds. Upon the table they set out some pelts, a basket of vegetables, baskets filled with packages of smoked and salted meats, and a basket of the bear meat. Around them were people trading all manner of goods. Farming equipment, baked goods, jewellery and trinkets, ales and meads, meats, vegetables, milk and eggs.

"Meat, vegetables and pelts for sale or trade," said Anzo in a loud voice.

"We've got fox, rabbit, and badger pelts. Sheep fleeces and cattle leathers," said Ruhsarr.

"Fresh bear meat. Fresh beef, mutton and lamb to sell or trade," said Anzo. By midday they had traded and sold most of their items.

Heidrich Graven approached the stall looking at the pelts.

"Anzo, Ruhsarr. Fine day to you," he said.

"And to you," said Anzo with a smile. "How are your family?"

"All very well, thank you. The children are growing up and helping more on the farm. Runo is big now and strong too. Una wants Theda to learn weaving, but the girl insists on working in the fields. She loves the land, that girl," said Heidrich.

"How old are they now?" said Anzo.

"Runo is twenty and Theda is eighteen. Both are of marrying age and Una is hoping for grandchildren before we get too old," said Heidrich. Anzo nudged Ruhsarr with his elbow and Ruhsarr looked back at him pointedly.

"I know what you mean. This one is nineteen now and it would be nice to know that I have someone to maintain the farm when I am gone," said Anzo.

"How are you two? I imagine things have been tough over the past few years," said Heidrich.

"Yes, since Aski was taken it has been, difficult. She was a wonderful wife and a good mother. The gods give and they take away. She must have been needed for other things in the next life. The farm is a lot of work without her, but we are getting by. It's been a little over two years and we are still trying to get back into the rhythm of the work again," said Anzo.

"I was so sad for you when she died. Everyone loved her, she always had a smile for everyone and wasn't afraid to get work done," said Heidrich.

"Thank you, Heidrich," Anzo Reached out and shook his hands." Your words mean a lot. Is there anything I can help you with today?" said Anzo.

"Can I have some of that bear meat and four Rabbit pelts. I have grain I can give you today," he said and patted the sack laid on his shoulder. "And I have breeding and milking cows for you at the farm. You will have to come and collect them though. Una's mother is arriving tomorrow, and I have to be there to meet her. You are more than welcome to stay for lunch. Both of you that is," said Heidrich. The two men shared a knowing look of an unspoken plan as Ruhsarr tied the bundle of meat with a leather strip and got a sack for the pelts.

"That would be great. We'll be there by midday. You're only part of a morning's walk away," said Anzo.

"Good. I'll see you both tomorrow," Heidrich said as he lifted the sack from his shoulder and handed it to Anzo and then took the items from Ruhsarr.

"You will indeed," said Anzo and smiled broadly.

By the end of the day they had traded all of their goods and were on their way home. The cart was now weighed down with sacs of grain, seeds, and farming tools. As they walked Yannee snorted and bobbed his head.

"Just a little further, old friend," said Anzo and he guided the heavy cart along.

"So, you intend for me to meet with Theda?" said Ruhsarr.

Anzo looked at him and smiled warmly.

"What makes you think that?" said Anzo in feigned surprise.

"Come on. You two couldn't have made it more obvious. Theda and I are both of marrying age and then suddenly we are going over to their farm tomorrow," said Ruhsarr.

"You are both of a good age to marry, and it's about time you took a wife. She is a pretty girl. She is also intelligent and hard working. Do you not like her?" said Anzo.

"I didn't mean that. Of course, she is lovely, and I would like to know her better," said Ruhsarr.

"What are you complaining about then? I'm not going to force you to marry her. I've simply set up a chance for you to get to know her that might not have happened of its own occurrence. You're still learning about life, my boy. Don't let opportunities pass you by, like with the bear for example," said

Anzo.

"Are you comparing Theda to a bear?" said Ruhsarr with a smile.

"No, you lump, I'm saying we took the opportunity. We had to move at just the right moment. If we hadn't, we would either have no bear, or we could have been the ones being eaten. If you let this opportunity to meet her pass you by she will find someone else," said Anzo.

Ruhsarr thought on this for a while as they walked.

"What if we don't like each other?" he said finally.

"I can't guarantee that you will, but you can't go through life wondering and not doing. You have to ask questions and put yourself in the right place at the right time. You have to give people the opportunity to say yes. If you don't the answer to all your unasked questions will always be no," said Anzo.

"I understand," said Ruhsarr.

"I know you do. You're smart, like your mother," said Anzo with a smile.

Chapter 4.

As the sun rose over the forest beyond their land Anzo opened his eyes and stood up from his straw filled sack bed. He pulled on his woollen woven clothes and pulled his deer skin over his shoulders. He nudged Ruhsarr who stirred and opened his eyes. As he got up and began to dress Anzo went to collect eggs and started a fire to make breakfast. Once the fire was established the two men sat and prepared strips of skewered bear meat. They placed them over the fire and turned them as the outer layers seared.

"I'm going to have a wash. I want to make myself presentable. I don't want Theda thinking I go around smelling of sheep shit all the time," said Ruhsarr.

"She lives and works on a farm. She knows what we do, she knows how we smell. She probably smells of sheep shit too," said Anzo.

Ruhsarr frowned at him.

"That isn't the point. I want to seem like I'm making an effort to smell like a human," he said. He picked up a woollen blanket and walked out through the door and out across the fields towards the nearby lake. Anzo smiled to himself.

"Good lad. We taught him well, Aski. He's growing up to be a fine young man," he said.

Ruhsarr stripped of his clothing and walked into the cool water up to his waist. He scrubbed at his body then dunked under the water and washed his hair. He walked back to the shore and dried himself and put on a clean set of clothing. As he headed back towards the house Anzo stepped out through the door. The older man had his axe strapped to his back. He handed Ruhsarr a coil of wound reed rope and a dagger. Ruhsarr took them, put the coil of rope over his shoulder and tucked the dagger in his belt.

"Are you ready to go? We have a good walk ahead of us," said Anzo.

"Yes. Let's go. Do we need to take Yannee?" said Ruhsarr.

"Yes. The cattle will follow him and if my knee starts playing up, I can get on his back. I'm not a young man anymore," said Anzo.

"You're not that old," said Ruhsarr and placed his hand on his dad's shoulder.

"I'm only a few years younger than Tuek the Elder," said Anzo.

"I take it back. Tuek is older than the mountains," said Ruhsarr with a laugh.

"Alright, there is no need to take the piss," said Anzo with a smile.

Ruhsarr stepped into the stable. When Yannee saw him, he nickered and nodded his head. Ruhsarr put the loop at the end of the rope over the horse's head and walked him out of the stable. The three of them began their journey along the well-worn path that led away from their farm.

After a good part of the morning spent walking they had just passed Aslakvaas and were on their way to the Graven's farm. They heard something high above them. The sound of something huge cutting through the air. They both looked up and saw the silhouette of a huge flying beast against the light sky. Its long, wide wings were splayed out and it soared though the warm morning sky with an air of majesty and grace. Its long, flat tail and long neck moved ever so slightly, constantly adjusting to steady its trajectory through the air. Its body was long and heavily muscled, and the late morning sun glinted off its orange scales. It let out a call. A deep, guttural sound that the two men on the ground could hear despite it being hundreds of feet above them. They watched it until it was out of sight over the horizon.

"Was that a dragon?" said Ruhsarr.

"Yes," said Anzo, in a short almost curt tone.

"Wow, I have never seen a dragon before," Ruhsarr said with a huge smile on his face.

"I don't like them. We should be careful," said Anzo with a serious expression.

"Are they really that bad?" said Ruhsarr with a frown.

"My grandfather lost his right arm and an eye to a dragon. They are extremely dangerous," said Anzo.

"What are we going to do?" said Ruhsarr.

"I don't know. Every so often they migrate to find a new home. Hopefully it will continue on its way and leave our land alone," said Anzo.

They continued walking and talking until they reached the border of the Graven's Farm. As they walked along the path towards the house in the centre of the land, Heidrich came out to meet them.

"Anzo. Ruhsarr. How are you? I hope your journey was swift and uneventful," he said.

"It was a fine walk. We saw a dragon though," said Anzo.

"A dragon you say. Well, hopefully it's just passing over and will leave us alone," said Heidrich.

"Aye," said Anzo.

"Are they really as destructive as my dad says?" said Ruhsarr.

"Oh yes. They are spoken of in high regards among the Elders. They are thought to bring fertile crops, good breeding of livestock, and successful hunting to whoever see them, but they are dangerous. My cousin had his entire farm burned to ash by a dragon. He lost everything. All of his land, along with two of his children. I do hope it doesn't choose to stay here. They are notoriously hard to get rid of. Once they take possession of a piece of land it is easier to abandon the surrounding area than try and move them along," said Heidrich.

"Hopefully it will just pass over then like you both say," said Ruhsarr.

"We'll keep watch for it, but for now the of two you must have worked up both a thirst and an appetite," he said.

"Yes," said the father and son.

"Come then, Una and Theda have made a stew, and we have some ale that has just become ready to drink this morn," said Heidrich.

"Sounds wonderful," said Anzo with a smile.

"Follow me," said Heinrich and returned the smile.

He led them across the fields where the cows and sheep grazed on the grass and into the house. Inside the long rectangular building that was very similar to their own with a stone lined fire in the middle. Above the fire stood a frame from which a large cooking pot hung. Inside the contents simmered and boiled. The air was warm and filled with the smell of freshly cooked food as a young woman stirred the stew. Ruhsarr looked at her and was taken aback by her beauty. She was tall and the glow from the fire played across her sun-kissed skin. She looked up over to him and swept her long blonde hair away from her large, jade green eyes. For a moment there was an expression of awe on her face and then a smile played across her full lips. Ruhsarr stood looking like a fool for a moment and then he smiled back at her.

"Ruhsarr, have you met my daughter, Theda. I believe you are around the same age," said Heidrich.

“I have seen her in the town, but we have never been introduced,” said Ruhsarr.

“Well, Ruhsarr, this is my daughter, Theda. Theda, this is Ruhsarr. His father, Anzo, owns the farm just beyond Aslakvaas,” said Heidrich.

“It’s a pleasure to meet you, Ruhsarr,” said Theda.

“A pleasure to meet you too, ma’am,” said Ruhsarr.

“You don’t have to ma’am me, Ruhsarr. I’m just a farmer’s daughter. Theda is enough,” she said and smiled.

“As you wish, Theda,” said Ruhsarr as he smiled.

“Well, Anzo and I have to discuss the cows I have available for trade. We’ll leave you two to get acquainted,” said Heidrich.

“Yes, we’ll see you two in a while,” said Anzo. The two men then made a hasty exit and left the two teens to talk.

“So, you live beyond Aslakvaas?” said Theda.

“Yes, our land borders with the forests of Haslow. That’s where we caught the bear,” said Ruhsarr.

“Ah, so that is where this meat came from. I was wondering where my father got it,” said Theda.

“Yes, we traded it to him at the market yesterday,” he said.

“How did you find the bear?” she said.

“It found us, well, our land I mean. We just followed its tracks. I wanted to move it along, but my dad said it needed to be killed. As we moved in on the bear it attacked him. If I hadn’t struck first, it would have killed him,” said Ruhsarr.

“So, it was you who felled the bear?” she said.

“Yes,” he said.

“I’m impressed. I can’t imagine fighting a bear. They are so big and scary. You are very brave,” she said.

"He was big and strong and tough. I had the upper hand though. He tried to attack me, but I struck him first. It was quick and clean. He died honourably," he said puffing out his chest and deepening his voice.

"Did you attack him with your ego," she said.

"No, with my axe. I know, I know, I'm not all pomp and bravado really," he said.

"I'm only joking. I really am impressed. We've put the meat in this stew. I can't wait to try it. It smells so nice," she said.

"It's good. We had some this morning for breakfast. You just have to make sure it's cooked well. Its predator meat so it's a bit denser than deer or beef," he said.

"I've cooked wolf before. It seems a lot like that so it's the first thing I started cooking when I got out of bed this morning," she said.

"Good, that's good," he said.

"Do you go hunting a lot?" she said.

"Yes, about once a week," he said.

"That must be fun. I want to go hunting with my father, but my mother won't allow it. She is scared I will be hurt. I keep telling her that I will be ok, but she won't listen," she said.

"You could come with me sometime if you like?" he said.

"I would like that," she said with a smile.

"How about the day after tomorrow?" he said and smiled back at her.

"Perfect," she said, still smiling.

The door opened and let in a slither of daylight as Theda's mother, Una, and grandma Greta walked into the house from the fields. They walked across the room and Greta set her sack of belongings down on the floor beside one of the straw beds. She walked over to Theda and kissed her on the cheek.

"Hello Grandma," said Theda.
"Hello dear. Who is your friend?" said Greta.
"This is Ruhsarr. He and his dad are here to collect some cattle in exchange for the bear meat in the stew," said Theda.
"Hello, Ruhsarr. I'm Greta, Theda's Grandma,"
"Hello, Greta. It's a pleasure to meet you," said Ruhsarr.
Greta leaned in close to Una.
"Looks like he's here for something else if you ask me," she whispered.
The two women giggled. Theda looked at Ruhsarr, her face flushed red, and he could feel himself blushing too.
"Ruhsarr and Anzo are staying for lunch," said Theda suddenly.
"Heinrich has already said as much. How is the stew coming along," said Una.
"It's ready to eat," said Theda.
"Good. Ruhsarr, be a dear and go and tell your dad and Heinrich to come and eat," said Una.
"Okay," said Ruhsarr.
He smiled at Theda and walked to the door and out into the fields. He found the two older men and Runo stood among the cows talking.
"This is Hannie. She is two years old and will be good for breeding and milking. Her mother, Samsi, is over here. She is ten years old but coming to the end of her breeding age. Both are strong and healthy, but I think Hannie will be best for you," said Heinrich as he patted Samsi on the neck.
"Thank you. Hannie will do fine. I have a bull she can breed with. When she starts producing offspring I'll share them with you," said Anzo.
"The stew is ready to eat when you're ready," said Ruhsarr as he approached them.
"Ah, wonderful. Just in time," said Heinrich.

"Thank you, son," said Anzo.
The four men walked back to the house where Heinrich led them inside. They all sat in a circle on the floor and Theda poured the stew into carved wooden bowls and passed them to the guests. Starting with her grandma, then Anzo and Ruhsarr. She passed bowls to Heinrich, Una, and Runo and then poured a bowl for herself. She sat down next to Ruhsarr as Una passed out small bread rolls. As they ate, they all talked. They told stories of their family's pasts, stories of the history of the land, and anecdotes of their own experiences.
When a few hours had passed Anzo nudged Ruhsarr and passed him his bowl. His son stacked it on top of his and passed them to Una.
"Thank you for the food. We must be on our way now to be home before nightfall," said Anzo.
"We thank you for coming. Thank you for the meat, without your bravery this meal would not have been possible," said Heinrich.
"You're welcome," said Anzo.
They all stood up as Heinrich and Runo walked them to the door.
"I'll help you ready Hannie for your journey," said Runo.
They walked out of the house and collected Yannee from the stable. Runo placed a harness around Hannie's head, and they all walked to the edge of the Graven's farmland.
"Thank you again," said Anzo.
"Thank you too," said Heinrich.
Theda briskly walked up to them and approached Ruhsarr.
"I was hoping to catch you before you left. I hope you have a safe journey, and I will see you soon, Ruhsarr," she leaned in and kissed him on the cheek.

Ruhsarr smiled and she held him with a lingering look before she turned and walked away.
Anzo and Heinrich looked at each other knowingly and chuckled.

"Farewell and a safe journey to you both," said Heinrich.

"Be well and see you soon," said Anzo.
The father and son then began the long walk home. It was a long Journey, and in spite of Ruhsarr's hopes for adventure, besides Anzo having to climb upon Yannee's back, it was largely uneventful. They got home shortly before the sun set. Ruhsarr guided the horse and cow into their stables. He got them and all the animals settled for the night. By the time he walked into their living area Anzo had built a fire and settled himself down. Ruhsarr sat down and took off his furs and clothing. He sat down in his bedding, gathered it around him, gazed into the flittering flames and his thoughts turned to Theda. That night he dreamt of her, that kiss and the prospects of seeing her again.

Chapter 5.

The next day Anzo and Ruhsarr woke up when the sun rose. They tended to the animals. Feeding and mucking them out. They worked the fields planting and harvesting crops. The day passed slowly and no matter what Ruhsarr did to pass the time the day just wouldn't go any faster. He walked through the field rounding up the sheep. He led the cows and the bull into their separate areas. Rounded up the chickens into their house. Finally he led Yannee into his stable. As he closed the door on the animal area his shoulders slumped. Anzo clapped a hand on his back.

"Don't worry, son. I know what it's like to wish the time away, but don't worry. Tomorrow will be here soon enough. Come on, it's time to eat," he said.

"Thanks dad," said Ruhsarr.

They went inside their house and Anzo set up the wood for a fire and lit it. Ruhsarr then set up he skewered bear meat by the flames while Anzo washed and cut up apples. They ate their supper and drank mead.

"What are your plans for tomorrow?" said Anzo.

"I'm taking Theda hunting. She hasn't been before so I'm going to take her hunting for deer," said Ruhsarr.

"You need to get some sleep then," said Anzo.

Ruhsarr rolled over onto his mattress and closed his eyes.

"Don't be in such a rush. You'll have many long years ahead of you," said Anzo.

"It feels like nothing is ever going to change," said Ruhsarr.

"I remember what it is like to be young. You feel like everything is taking so long and you want things to happen. Well, one day you will look back and realise how much time you had ahead of you. You should cherish these days. They are the ones you will remember when you get to be an old man, like me," said Anzo.

"You're not that old," said Ruhsarr.

"I'm old enough," said Anzo.

"Old enough for what?" said Ruhsarr.

Anzo smiled to himself.

"To have learned a few lessons. Like being careful what I wish for. I know you want adventure. One day you will look back and realise how much things have change, and that you yourself have also changed. Tomorrow will be a good day. You will see. It will be a day to remember," said Anzo.

"I hope so. Good night, dad," said Ruhsarr.

"Good night, son," said Anzo.

The next morning Ruhsarr was up and dressed before the sun rose. He packed some fruits and dried meats into his bag. Wrapped his bow and sixteen arrows into a sheep skin that he then tied at both ends and hung over his shoulder. He strapped his axe to his back then tucked his knife into his belt. He then went into the animal area, let Yannee out of his stable, and walked him out into the fresh morning air. He folded the thick blanket, threw it over the horse, and climbed onto his back.

"Forward, boy," he said and clicked his tongue. Yannee began to walk along the path away from the house.

"Away," said Ruhsarr.

Soon they were galloping among the trees and through meadows towards the Graven farm. An hour and a half later he arrived at the edge of the farmland and slowed to a gentle trot. Heinrich was tending to his crops and watched as Ruhsarr and

Yannee arrived. He stood up straight and waved to them. Ruhsarr raised his hand in response.

"Good morning, Ruhsarr. What brings you here?" said Heinrich.

"I'm here to take Theda to pick some flowers," said Ruhsarr.

Heinrich eyed the sheep skin and axe on Ruhsarr's back.

"Tell me. Why do you need to be armed to pick flowers?" said Heinrich.

"For protection, sir. You never know when you may run into goblin men and wild beasts. And with the arrival of the dragon about these lands I would hate to take your daughter out without any means of protecting her. If the need should arise," said Ruhsarr.

"Aye, aye. That be true. You're a clever one aren't you," said Heinrich.

"I like to say that I'm strong of arm and strong of brain too, sir" said Ruhsarr.

"Mhmm," Heinrich grunted.

Theda ran across the field towards them. She wrapped her arms around Heinrich and kissed him on the cheek.

"Good morning, father. Ruhsarr is taking me to the meadow to pick flowers. How lovely is he," she said.

Heinrich looked from Theda to Ruhsarr and back to Theda suspiciously.

"Ok you two. Have fun and be safe. I'm entrusting her safety onto you, Ruhsarr son of Anzo," he said.

"Yes, sir. I will return her to you unscathed," said Ruhsarr.

"See that you do," said Heinrich.

Ruhsarr helped Theda up onto Yannee's back and they rode off in the direction of the forest.

They rode along a well-trodden path through a meadow. Theda had her arms wrapped around Ruhsarr's waist and she held on tight. The feeling of her body pressed against his stirred feelings of longing within him.

"So, where are we going?" she said.

"There is a clearing over this hill. Three herds of deer live around this area and come here to graze," he said.

"So, are you going to show me how to hunt them?" she said.

"That's right. We'll stop just over here, and I'll show you how to set up the bow," he said.

"Hey up," he said and pulled on the reins. Yannee slowed to a stop and the pair climbed off his back. Ruhsarr threw the end of the rope from the horse's head harness around a tree and tied it. He stroked the flack of the horse's neck.

"Stay here, boy. We'll be back soon," he said. Yannee grunted as if he understood.

Ruhsarr then turned and smiled at Theda. He scanned the ground and found what he was looking for.

"Look there at the ground," he said to Theda and pointed to what he had seen, "You see where the soil and grass are disturbed. The little hoof prints. Those are deer tracks. They lead in that direction through the forest towards the clearing. We are going to follow them. Just follow my lead and we'll see what we can catch," he said.

"Oh, I can't wait," she said and took hold of his arm.

After ten minutes they came to the clearing in the trees. A large irregularly shaped opening where only grass and flowers grew. Ruhsarr stopped and Theda stopped behind him.

"Look," said Ruhsarr and pointed into the centre of the clearing.
"The deer," she said.
"Yes," he said.
"What do we do now?" she said.
"We need to get down and get in closer," he said. He knelt down, she followed his lead, and they crawled closer. They stopped behind a fallen tree and knelt up behind it.
"You've shot a bow before, haven't you?" he said.
"Yes, I've shot turnips for practice, and I've shot at foxes. The turnip was easy but I'm yet to hit a fox," she said.
"Ok well, this is no different. You just to relax and choose your target," he said and passed her the bow.
She held it tight and took her position. She then lined up the notch in the end of the arrow to the string and pulled it back.
"Choose your target," he said as he moved up next to her and looked over her shoulder so he could see where she was aiming. "The big buck?" he said.
"Yes, she said.
"Ok, breathe in slowly and as you breathe out release the arrow," he said.
She drew in a deep breath in and Ruhsarr pretended not to notice as her chest heaved.
"When you're ready. Just take your time," he whispered.
She began to breathe out and released the arrow. As it sliced through the air neither of them noticed the trees shudder around them. The arrow hit its mark piercing the buck's heart and killing it instantly. Blood gushed from its nostrils, and it dropped to the grass and moss-covered ground. The other deer nearby began to run. Theda sat still for a moment as a smile spread over her lips.
"I got him," she whispered.

She turned, hugged Ruhsarr and planted a kiss on his lips. Ruhsarr was taken aback for a moment but then kissed her. They smiled at each other.

"You're a natural at this," he said.

"It's got to be beginners' luck," she said.

"Maybe, but you hit it perfectly. Be proud of yourself," he said.

"I am. I can't wait to show my mum," she said.

"Let's go and collect it. The smell of blood will draw nearby predators," he said.

They got too their feet and climbed over the fallen tree. As they stepped towards the clearing the air swirled around them. Dust and leaves were drawn up into the air. The huge thump and whoosh of wings beating the air down filled their ears. They stopped in their tracks as the long, heavy body of the beast descended into the clearing. The sun gleamed off its orange scales like fire. It maintained its position and flapped its wings so that it hovered there for a moment while it looked down at the buck. It drew in its wings and dropped through the gap in the trees and landed with an impact that shook the ground beneath Ruhsarr and Theda's feet. It folded its wings down, took a few steps forwards, and picked up the buck in its enormous front paws. Each had four digits. Each digit was tipped with dagger length claws.

"Hey, that's ours!" said Ruhsarr.

The dragon raised its head from its prize to look at them. Its pale green eyes looked out from its long narrow head. There was a fan of horns the length of a human arm angle backwards over the crown of its skull. It opened its jaws and made a series of vocal noises.

"Hukarrr Rambassk adk faaaaarrrr."

To Ruhsarr and Theda they sounded like words, but it was a language neither of them had ever heard.

It turned its head back to the buck and bit into it. The beak-like snout sliced through the flesh with ease.

"Hey!" shouted Theda.

The dragon drew its head back and lifted a chunk from the carcass. It flicked its head back and opened its blood covered jaws. The lump of flesh fell further into its mouth. It snapped its jaw shut and swallowed. It looked back at the two humans and took a step towards them. Ruhsarr took Theda's hand, and they ran back into the forest in the direction they had come from.

They heard the dragon following them but soon it had flown over them and they both slowed their pace. Ruhsarr fell to the floor panting and Theda fell down next to him. They caught their breath. They were both overcome with emotion, laughing and crying at the same time.

"What were we thinking?! That was the dragon. We just got robbed by a dragon," he said.

"I can't believe it took my deer," she said.

"It could have taken us, quite easily," he said.

A smile played across her face.

"Do not worry yourself. I would have defended you," she said.

"Really? What would you have done if it had grabbed me?" he said.

"I would have lunged at it like this," she said, and threw herself on him. They both fell back, and their eyes met. They kissed each other. She caressed his wide shoulders as she lay on top of him. His hands slid down to the small of her back and he pulled her close. She kissed his mouth and then pushed him back.

"We shouldn't, I mean, I want to, and I really like you, but we're only supposed to be picking flowers," she said.

"You're right. Let's just take things at a steady pace," he said.
He stood up and helped her to her feet. They looked into each other's eyes again. Their mouths were inches apart.

"Flowers," they both said and laughed.

"Flowers, flowers, flowers," he said.

"Some nice, lovely flowers. Just flowers," she said.
He took her by the hand, and they began to walk back to the place they had left Yannee.

The horse was getting restless when they arrived. His ears were stood up and he was blasting loud snorts from his nostrils. Ruhsarr slowly ran his hand down the horse's neck.

"Hey, hey. Relax, big man. It's ok. It's all ok," he whispered next to the horse's ear.
He untethered the harness from the tree and lead Yannee into a nearby meadow. Here they picked some flowers and wrapped them in a woollen shawl. Yannee strolled around sniffing and tasting the ones he found interesting. Ruhsarr took his bow from his back.

"What are you doing?" said Theda.

"We might as well take something home with us," he said lining up an arrow.
She looked where he was aiming and saw a rabbit pop its head up just as he released the arrow. It was a direct hit, and the rabbit was dead before it fell. He and Theda got another three between them. They tied the hind feet together with twine and Ruhsarr hung them over his shoulder. He climbed onto Yannee's back and helped Theda climb up and sat her behind him.

"Walk on," said Ruhsarr.
Yannee turned his attention away from the tasty flowers and strode in the direction of Theda's home.

They arrived back at the Graven farm in the early afternoon. They were greeted by Heinrich and Runo as they climbed down from Yannee's back.

"Welcome back. How was your flower picking trip," said Runo with a smirk.

"Lovely, we picked some lovely flowers," said Theda and smiled sweetly.

"And what did you catch?" said Heinrich.

"What do you mean?" said Theda,

"Come on, you know exactly what I mean. You went hunting. I don't mind, just don't tell your mother. She worries too much about you," said Heinrich.

"We caught some rabbits. We did shoot a deer too, but we lost it," said Theda.

"What do you mean, you lost it? Did it get away?" said Heinrich.

"Yes," said Ruhsarr quickly. "It was a long shot and although the arrow hit the deer it didn't kill it and the animal got away,"

Theda gave him a stern look, but he took her hand in his and raised his eyebrows pleadingly. *I hope you know what you are* doing her eyes said.

"That's a shame. We could have done with the meat and the pelt," said Runo.

"I know. We all could have benefitted from the catch but that's just the way it goes sometimes. You should have the rabbits though. You have more mouths to feed here," said Ruhsarr.

"Thank you," said Heinrich.

"Thank you for allowing me to spend the day with your lovey daughter, sir," said Ruhsarr.

"The pleasure was all mine," said Heinrich.

"I should be going now. I only have a few more hours before sunset," said Ruhsarr and twitched Yannee's reins.

The horse shook his head and huffed a breath for his nostrils.

"Ok, say hello to your dad from me," said Heinrich.

"I will," said Ruhsarr.

"I'll walk you to the edge of our land," said Theda.

She took his hand and both of them and the horse walked to the edge of the Graven's farmlands.

"Why did you lie about the dragon?" she said.

"I panicked," said Ruhsarr.

"You panicked?" she repeated.

"I desperately want to see you again. If we told them the truth your dad would never let me take you out again. Let alone your mum. I hope it was just a coincidence that it was in the same place we were for it to steal the buck," he said.

"Oh Ruhsarr. That is all you had to say. I understand now why you didn't tell them. You can come and take me out again. We'll go hunting again in a few days. If we see the dragon again though we need to tell someone," she said with a smile.

He leaned closer to her, and they kissed deeply.

"Yes, I promise," he said.

"Go on now. You better set off," she said.

He held her close, and they kissed again and then he climbed onto Yannee's back and rode away.

As Theda watched him she could feel the first embers of love igniting in her heart. She had a good feeling about Ruhsarr. He was a good man, if a little reckless. She liked that though, he was wild and free, but strong willed and intelligent.

Over the next few weeks they went out again hunting and fishing. They even picked flowers and lay together in a field watching the clouds pass over head. Their love grew and blossomed and Ruhsarr began to make plans.

Chapter 6.

Ruhsarr rode up to the Graven's farmland. He dismounted his horse and walked to the farmhouse. As he got there Heinrich stepped out of the house. He walked up to the younger and smiled.

"Ruhsarr, good morning. How are you," he said with a smile.

"Good morning Heinrich. I'm well, thank you. How are you, sir," said Ruhsarr.

"Good, I'm good. Here to see Theda, I assume?" said Heinrich.

"Actually, I was hoping I could talk to you for a moment," said Ruhsarr.

"Oh, ok. What do you want from me?" said Heinrich.

Ruhsarr suddenly seemed a little nervous.

"I, well, as you have noticed me and Theda have been spending a lot of time together," said Ruhsarr.

"Yes, I have noticed. She is fond of you," said Heinrich.

"That is the thing. I'm not just fond of her, I love her. I want to marry her, obviously with your permission," said Ruhsarr.

Heinrich fixed the younger man with a stare and furrowed his brow.

"You want to marry my daughter?" he said.

"Erm…yes, sir. If you would allow it," said Ruhsarr.

Heinrich continued to stare and Ruhsarr felt his face flush red. Heinrich raised his eyebrows and his face broke into a broad smile.

"Of course you can. You have my blessing. The joining of our two families will be highly beneficial to both. Just one thing," said Heinrich.

"Yes, sir?" said Ruhsarr.

"Ask her too. I have raised my children to be strong willed and know their own minds. So it is ultimately her choice. I won't force her, and neither will you. Is that understood?" said Heinrich.

"Yes sir. Loud and clear. I would not force her to do anything she doesn't want to do. Her tenacity is one of the things I love about her," said Ruhsarr.

"I'm glad to hear that," said Heinrich.

At that moment Theda stepped out of the house and approached them. Both men smiled at her. She threw her arms around her dad and kissed him on the cheek.

"Good morning, dad. Me and Ruhsarr are going to catch fish and maybe some birds today," she said.

"I know, we have just been talking about the best parts of the river to visit," said Heinrich.

"I hope he told you some good spots. When we were kids he took us to a place that we now know is near an Imp cave. We spent most of the day trying to stop them stealing our bait and spears. All the while he found it hilarious," she said with a smile.

Heinrich Looked at Ruhsarr and smiled.

"I was teaching them a lesson in trust. Just because someone tells you something is good doesn't necessarily mean that it's true. Also, people can play pranks," he said.

"Those are good lessons to learn," said Ruhsarr with a smile.

"Don't encourage him," said Theda as she took Ruhsarr's hand in hers.

"We should be on our way. We have a good part of the morning's travelling to do to get to the fishing spot," said Ruhsarr as he climbed onto Yannee's back.

"Ok, be careful and have fun, and remember what I told you, Ruhsarr," said Heinrich.

“I will. Thank you sir,” said Ruhsarr and helped Theda onto the horse.

They waved to Heinrich as they rode away from the farm. Soon they were riding through the meadows and forests far beyond the farmlands. They reached the river and followed it for a few miles talking as they went. Theda taught Ruhsarr songs that her grandma had taught her as a child. She wrapped her arms around his waist and squeezed him tight. He placed his hand over hers and enjoyed the warmth and shape of her body pressing against his back. The trees were dense and very little sunlight made it down to the forest floor. He pulled on the reins and Yannee slowed to a walk. They reached an area clear of trees where the river curved around a rocky outcrop. They stopped and Ruhsarr dismounted from the horse. Here the water grew deep as it surged around the bend. In the clear water fish swam hurriedly against the current, dodging and flitting over and around each other.

“This is the place,” he said and climbed down from the horse.

“It’s amazing. I’ve never even seen this place before. How did you find it?” she said as she swung her leg over and dropped down beside him.

“My great grandad found it years ago. We have kept it as a family secret obviously because it’s good for fishing. We’re deep in the forest here, far beyond our lands. Beyond the reaches that most people are willing to travel. That’s how we have kept it secret for so long. We are alone here,” he said and winked.

He attached Yannee’s harness to a tree. The horse shook his main and reached his head towards the grassy forest floor where the sunlight reached. He then happily began to munch at the delicious fresh shoots. Ruhsarr took two spears from the items packed onto the horses back.

"Are we safe to be here?" she asked suddenly looking a little concerned.

"Yes. Not even the Goblin men venture this deep into the forest. Forest Folk live in the caves around here. They will be ok with us as long as we are loving and respectful to their land. We also have to leave them half our catch," he said.

"What would happen if we didn't?" she said.

"My grandad told me his cousin refused to leave any fish one time. The only parts of him that was ever found was his two front teeth," he said.

Theda raised her eyebrows in shock.

"Yep, you always leave half your catch, or you don't leave," he said.

"Half the catch. Seems fair," she said.

They approached the river side and crouched down. As the looked into the water fish tumbled over each other and broke the surface.

"This is incredible. I don't think I have ever seen so many fish," she said.

"These are the adults. We can take a few but only enough to feed our family. Too much will anger the Forest Folk," he said.

"So we just spear them. This won't take long," she said.

She jabbed the spear into the water and pulled it back empty. She jabbed again but still caught nothing.

"Not that easy is it," he said with a smile.

"No, how are they able to dodge my spear?" she said.

"It's just because they are so fast. Try again. There is no trick, you just have to hope," he said.

"Hope for what?" she said.

"That your spear tip and a fish are in the same place at the same time," he said with a smile.

"That's helpful," she said with a frown.

Ruhsarr tried to keep the smile from his face.

"It's just the truth. Go on, you might get one this time," he said and motioned for her to try again.

She thrust her spear into the water. This time it came back with the flapping body of a fish two feet in length skewered on the end.

"I got one, I got one!" she said as elated as the first time she had caught a fish as a child.

"See, you're getting the hang of it. Well done," he said.

She grabbed him and pulled him close then kissed him. They hugged and danced around by the water's edge.

"Come on let's try for a few more," he said.

An hour later they had six fish lay in two piles and wrapped in a cloth to keep them clean.

As they packed away their things she looked at him.

"Seeing as this spot is a family secret, what will your dad say now that I know?" she said.

"I have been thinking about that," he said as he took her in his arms and held her close.

"Really?" she said and smiled.

"Yes, Theda, I brought you here to ask you if you will…if you will be my wife?" he said.

Her smile grew even broader, and tears welled in her eyes.

"Yes. Yes, Ruhsarr, I will be your wife," she said.

He squeezed her tight and they kissed. She pulled him down to the grass covered earth and kissed him again as they lay down. He ran his hands over her shoulder and slid the rough fabric of her dress away from the soft skin of her chest. He then kissed her neck, and she gasped in his ear. Her skin raised into gooseflesh at the touch of his lips. She slid her hands up his shirt and caressed is abdomen until her fingers found his chest. He knelt up and roughly pulled away his clothing. His body was strong and defined from working the field. Her eyes lingered over the muscular structure of his chest and shoulders. She looked down to his abdominal muscles and down to his pelvis. He was hard and ready, and she felt a longing that spread through every inch of her body.

"I want you, Ruhsarr. I want you inside me," she said as she pulled up her skirt and spread her legs. He moved and positioned himself between her thighs. As they looked into each other's eyes he slid into her. She gasped as they moved together. Feeling the heat and the taught muscles of each other's bodies slide against each other. They had both wanted each other from the first moment they had met. Now, as they made love they both knew that they had found the person they needed. He shuddered slightly and throbbed inside her. She moaned as the rhythmical movement brought her to orgasm. He threw his head back and growled with euphoric pleasure as he climaxed. He buried his head in her neck, panting and they both lay still for a moment. She hugged him then he rolled and lay down beside her. They kissed and smiled at each other.

"I love you, my wife," he said.

"And I love you too, my husband," she said. They lay in each other's arms for a while longer. Ruhsarr stood up and dressed and then reached his hand out. She took it and he helped her to her feet. They collected their belongings and fishing spears. They walked back to the tree where Yannee was now lay down. He watched as they approached and then raised his head. As Ruhsarr untied the reins from the tree the horse shook his head and huffed.

He then used some twine to tie one of the packages of fish to the same tree. He helped Theda onto the horse and then climbed on himself. Theda saw movement among the trees from the corner of her eye. As she looked towards the area she saw many pairs of bright turquoise eyes looking at her. The more she looked the more she could see. Ten, fifteen, twenty, maybe even as many as thirty pairs of eyes. Ruhsarr clicked his tongue and Yannee began to walk along the path away from the river. As he began to canter and they went deeper into the forest Theda looked back. A tall woman with long, black, braided hair, marbled grey skin, and dressed in brown and green clothing unfastened the package from the tree. She held it out infront of her, then pulled it close to her chest, nodded her head and smiled. Theda waved and turned to face forwards again.

"Always leave half the catch for the Forest Folk," said Ruhsarr already knowing what she had seen.

They arrived back at the Graven's farm and Theda jumped down from the horse before Ruhsarr had him to a complete stop. She ran to her father as he stepped out of the door and hugged him. She was smiling so wide that her cheeks ached and tears of joy ran down her face.

"He asked me. He asked me to marry him!" she said.

"And what did you say, child?" said Heinrich.

"Yes! I said yes!" she said.

Hearing all the commotion and sounds of excitement outside Una came out from her home.

"What's going on?" she said.

"Ruhsarr asked me to marry him, and I said yes," said Theda.

Una smiled herself and tears welled in her eyes as she held her arms out to her daughter. Theda released Heinrich and took her mother up a tight hug. They laughed and rocked from side to side. As Ruhsarr climbed down from the horse's back Heinrich smiled and took him by the hand.

"Welcome into the family, son," he said.

"Thank you," said Ruhsarr and pulled him into a hug.

"Will you stay and eat or are you going home to tell your father the good news?" said Heinrich.

"I'll come in and help cook. We have fish. Then I'll be on my way," said Ruhsarr.

"Good, good. Put Yannee in the stable and then come inside," said Heinrich.

When the horse was safely stowed with the other animals, Ruhsarr walked into the house.

"Come in and sit down, Ruhsarr. We have mead and cheese. The fish is ready to be cooked," said Heinrich.

Ruhsarr sat down next to Theda, and she wrapped her arms around him and place her cheek against his shoulder. She passed him the fish that she had gutted. He took the knife, cut off the head and tail and sliced the body in two. He then skewered the two sides and placed them over the fire. Heinrich, Una and Runo had prepared the other two fish in the same way.

"Tell us, Ruhsarr, where you found such fine fish," said Una.

Ruhsarr smiled and as they ate he told them the story of the place in the forest where the river runs thick with fish.

"Are the Forest folk safe to be around?" said Una.

"They don't come near unless you step onto their lands and don't keep your side of a bargain," said Ruhsarr.

"Can you direct us to this place?" said Heinrich.

"Unfortunately not. I can only show people who bare my family name. That was part of the bargain," said Ruhsarr.

Ruhsarr wrapped the last portion of fish in a clean cloth for Anzo. They all made their way outside and hugs were exchanged all round. Heinrich drew a knife from his belt and placed it into Theda's hands. She looked at the long iron blade and bone handle that was calved into the head of a bull.

"It belonged to your grandfather. He told me to give it to you when you got married," said Heinrich.

"Thank you. I will keep it with me as long as I live," said Theda.

"Look at this, Ruhsarr. Isn't it beautiful," she said. Ruhsarr looked at the knife and admired the craftsmanship. He then looked at Heinrich.

"Your father was very skilled," he said.

"Thank you, Ruhsarr. He would have appreciated that," said Heinrich with a smile.

Ruhsarr then stepped into the stable and brought out Yannee. He climbed onto the horse's back and helped Theda up and she settled in behind him. The family waved to them as they set off back towards his farm.

Upon arriving back at his home they dismounted the horse and led him into the stables. They walked around the of the outside house and as they reached the door Anzo opened it and greeted them.

"Was your hunt successful?" he said.

"It was. We caught some fish. We cooked it and we have some for you," said Ruhsarr and handed him the package of food.

"Nice. I was about to start cooking but this is great. Thank you," said Anzo, he looked at Theda. "Will you come in and eat with us? I would be glad of the company."

"Thank you, I've already eaten my share, but we will come in," she said.

Anzo smiled and stepped aside so they could enter. They all sat down and talked as they passed around a bladder of mead. Anzo opened the package and his expression changed for a smile to a frown. He eyed it for a moment. He took a piece of the meat between his fingers and held it there for a moment. He put it to his nose and sniffed it. He then placed it in his mouth, chewed, and swallowed it.

"Where did you catch this fish," he said and stared at Ruhsarr.

"From the river in the forest," said Ruhsarr.

"The spot in the Forest Folk's land?" said Anzo.

"Yes," said Ruhsarr.

"How many times have I told you, you can't take anyone who isn't a member of our family!" said Anzo as he slammed his fist against the floor. "Do you have any idea what you have done?!"

"Dad, it's ok," said Ruhsarr.

"How is it ok? How is this ok?! You don't mess with the Forest Folk!" roared Anzo.

"I asked Theda to marry me, and she accepted my proposal. She is part of our family now," said Ruhsarr.

Anzo's eyes widened and his brow raised from its furrowed position and his lips turned up from a frown back into a smile of relief.

"Ruhsarr! You should have started with that. This is fantastic," he said as he got to his feet and pulled his son up and hugged him.

"Fantastic," he repeated. "Please tell me you left half your catch,"

“Of course, I’m not completely stupid,” said Ruhsarr.

“I know, I know. Congratulations,” said Anzo. He then pulled Theda into a big strong hug too.

“Congratulations, my new daughter. I am so happy for you both. Sit, let us drink more mead. This is a celebration,” he said.

They drank late into the night, and all passed out around the fire.

Chapter 7.

As the morning light illuminated the gaps between the door and its frame, Theda opened her eyes. Ruhsarr's muscular arms were wrapped around her. She looked up at him and smiled. He stirred, stretched, and slowly opened his eyes. He smiled back at her, and they held each other tight.

"Good morning, my Ruhsarr," she said.

"Good morning, Theda," he said in a hoarse voice. She snuggled into his shoulder and kissed his neck. He moved his head and kissed her on the cheek. She adjusted her position a little and kissed his mouth. Across from them on the other side of the fire Anzo stirred and rolled over. He opened his eyes and looked over at them then rolled back over and stood up. Theda buried he face in Ruhsarr's shoulder and smiled. Anzo wrapped himself in clothing and furs and walked to the door.

"Sorry," said Ruhsarr.

"No need to apologise. I'll give you two some privacy," said Anzo.

He then opened the door and stepped out into the cool morning air. He closed the door behind him and the two newlyweds giggled.

"Where were we?" said Theda.

"Right here," said Ruhsarr as he rolled her onto her back and kissed her.

Anzo walked to the stream and knelt down at its edge. He took a small wooden bowl from his satchel and dunked it into the water. He raised the vessel to his lips and tipped his head back as he poured it into his mouth. He opened his eyes and high above him a dragon was silhouetted against the clouds. He jumped up to his feet and watched as it turned to the left and began to descend. He ran into his wheat field and watch where it was headed. It circled over the forest in the northern section of his land. All the time descending towards the crest for a large hill which stood out high above the forest canopy. It slowly came down to land, flapping its enormous wings until Anzo lost sight of it.

"No, No! Not on my land! Not my land!" said Anzo aloud to himself.

Without thinking he ran into the forest.

As he made his way through the trees and undergrowth birds and animals ran past him in the opposite direction. Even a pack of wolves ran past him but paid no attention to him at all. Soon the forest around him was eerily quiet. As he approached the hill the deep booming roar of the dragon rang out over the forest. Anzo dropped to his knees behind a boulder and covered his ears with his hands. The roar was followed by three language-like vocalisations. They were definitely words but like nothing Anzo had ever heard before. When he was sure that the beast had stopped its outburst he looked out around the side of the rock. Being careful to not give away his location. The dragon was stood up straight on its back legs on the plateau of the hill. It held it wings out and to full span and was looking out across the horizon. Clearly a display of some kind. To Anzo it looked like a warning to ward off any other nearby dragons. When it was happy that nothing was going to dispute its warning it dropped back down on to all four legs and folded its wings down onto its back. It then began to descend the hill. Anzo felt his heart begin to beat more rapidly than it already was.

Had it seen him? Would these be his final moments?

He felt a huge relief when the beast stopped at the mouth of a cave and stepped inside. He took this moment to slip away as he remained unnoticed.

Back at the farm Ruhsarr and Theda heard the dragon's roar and ran out into the fields. Upon finding them empty and no signs of Anzo they had begun to frantically search for him.

"He's not in the wheat field or in the grazing fields," said Ruhsarr as he walked back towards the house.

"He's not by the stream over by the lake either. What are we going to do?" said Theda.

"We need to ride to Aslakvaas. We need to warn them that the dragon has landed on our land," said Ruhsarr.

They dressed in heavy clothing and furs, then got Yannee ready for the journey. Just as they were walking him out from the stables. Anzo came running out from the treeline. He was breathing heavily as he moved fast on weary legs.

"It's landed…the dragon…has… landed," he said between panting breaths.

Ruhsarr caught him under the arms as the older man stumbled the last few steps.

"It landed… The monster…wants our land… It's landed…and it's trying to claim…our land!" said Anzo.

"Catch your breath," said Ruhsarr.

Anzo nodded his head and took long deep breaths. Soon his heart rate was returning to normal, and his breath were becoming more even.

"We heard its roar. Did you follow it?" said Ruhsarr.

"Yes. I ran to the hill. I saw it land," said Anzo. He heaved himself up from the ground.

"Are you crazy? It could have killed you!" said Ruhsarr.

"Maybe so, but I had to see where it was making its lair," said Anzo as he checked Yannee's harness and looked him over.

“Why? Why be so reckless?” said Ruhsarr.

“Because now when we get a team together to chase it off we won’t have to waste time trying to find it,” said Anzo.

“Woah. Hold on. Chase it off? This isn’t a bear we’re talking about. It’s a dragon. We need to leave this place,” said Ruhsarr.

Anzo stepped close so that is face was inches from his son.

“Listen to me and listen well. This farm has been in our family since the forest was mere saplings. We dig these fields and raise animals here in the same way our elders did when the sun sparked into light. Besides, you and this place are all I have left of my Aski. I promised her I would raise you here. I promised I would let nothing take this place from us. I promised her as she lay dying in my arms, and I don’t intend to break my promise. Not for anyone, or anything,” he said and pointed towards the hill in the distance.

Tears welled in Ruhsarr’s eyes, and he nodded his head.

“Ok dad,” said Ruhsarr humbly.

Theda hugged Ruhsarr’s arm. He looked at her and then back at Anzo.

“Let’s go and get that team together,” he said.

With that they set out on the path to Aslakvaas.

Chapter 8.

They approached the outer wooden walls of Aslakvaas town just before midday. They could see that the gates were closed as they got closer. Anzo stepped forwards and knocked on them. The guard looked down over the wall and saw him.

"Anzo, it's good to see you. You're early though. The market isn't for another two days," said he said.

"I'm not here for the market. I need to speak to the town elders. It's a matter of urgency," said Anzo.

"You have arrived at the right time. They are holding a council meeting in the Elder's Hall," said the guard.

He disappeared down behind the wall and the gate opened. Anzo, Ruhsarr, and Theda walked into the town and the guard close the gate behind them. The entire town was built on a light gradient that rose into a hill in the centre. On top of the hill stood the Elder's Hall. A large, stone, rectangular building with thick walls and a tall, wooden roof that overhung the walls and almost touched the ground. They climbed the hill and tied Yannee's reins to a trough of hay to the left of the heavy wooden doors. These stood in the centre of the front wall.

"What do we do?" said Ruhsarr.

"Leave it to me. I've known all these people since I was a child," said Anzo.

He took his dagger from his belt and hammered the pommel against a circle of metal in the middle of the right door. The sound reverberated loud into the building. From within they heard the voice of an older man say "Enter." Anzo pushed the door open and the three of them entered the building.

The air in the building was thick with the scent of animals and burning herbs. Wooden struts supported the high roof at evenly spaced positions. In the centre there stood a circle of tall, painted, monolithic stones. These surrounded an alter which held offerings of food and mead. They walked past the circle of stones and at the far end of the building five people sat behind a long table. The older man sat in the middle called to them.

"Anzo, my friend. It's good to see you. It has been a long time since you have ventured into our hall," said the man with a smile on his face.

"It is good to see you too, Tuek. This is my son, Ruhsarr and my daughter in law, Theda," said Anzo.

"Good day to you both," said Tuek. "To my right are Elders Drassi and Heg. To my left are Elders Golm and Vito."

"Good day, my Elders," the three farmers said. Slowly the smile faded from Tuek's face and was replaced by a frown.

"Why are you here, Anzo? Your presence in this sacred building makes me assume that there is a grim reason for your company," he said.

"Aye. The last time I stood before you in this building it was to tell you of the passing of my Aski. Today I bring news that not only affects me and my family, but all the families of this village. I have come here to ask, and if need beg for your help," said Anzo.

He then waited for the Elders to confer. They look back and fore and muttered among themselves for a moment then Tuek looked to Anzo.

"You may proceed," he said.

"We Miehyelzah's have owned the lands just south of here for as long as the memories in song and stories can recall. My family have worked the fields from wild earth to good food bearing, animal rearing land. We have fended off intruders both human, animal, Forest Folk, and even goblin men. Now though my land and the land it stands upon, the land of this town, has been invaded by something that I cannot repel or bear arms against by myself. A dragon has settled in the forest and in doing so I believe it is attempting to claim this area as its own. This causes problems not just for me, but for all of us here in these lands. I have come before you to ask that you allow me to assemble a team to drive away or, if need be, kill this beast," said Anzo.

"You want to take a group of our warriors into your forest to hunt a dragon?" said Elder Drassi.

"That is my request, my elder," said Anzo.

"This is a dangerous expedition you will be taking our people on. One from which they may not return," she said

"It is true, I cannot guarantee their safe return, but the price we all shall pay of we do nothing is much greater than the lives of several men," said Anzo.

"Allow us to confer on this matter. We will send a messenger when we have reached our decision," said Elder Heg.

"Thank you. May the gods smile upon you," said Anzo.

"And may the Gods smile upon you," said the Elders in unison.

Anzo then turned and began to walk back to the doors.

"Where are you going? What about their decision?" said Ruhsarr as he strode after his father.

"That is all we can do for now. They will reach their decision in a day, maybe two," said Anzo.

"But we need an answer," said Ruhsarr.

"And we will get one, in a day or two," said Anzo and kept on walking.

"But…" said Ruhsarr.

"No buts," said Anzo cutting him off. They need to confer with those of different planes. It takes…" said Anzo.

"A day or two?" said Theda.
"Yes," said Anzo as he looked at her and smiled. Ruhsarr threw up his hands in frustration and resignation and walked after them.
They unfastened Yannee's reins and headed for Theda's family farm.

A few hours later they arrived and were greeted by an extremely happy Heinrich. He approached them with a big smile and his arms held out. Theda ran towards him and fell into his arms and hugged him tight.
"How are you, my child?" said Heinrich.
"I'm well. We celebrated with Anzo last night. Sadly, we have bad news today," said Theda.
"Oh dear. I hope you are all well," said Heinrich. Theda nodded a looked up at him with mournful eyes.
Anzo stepped closer.
"Though we are all well, my land has unfortunately been invaded by the dragon we spotted a few weeks ago," he said.
Heinrich's eyes grew wide, and his jaw hung slack.
"The dragon is in your fields?!" he said after a few moments.
"Not in my fields but in my forest. We have just been to speak with the village elders and asked for their help. We are now waiting for their decision," said Anzo.
"I can see no reason why they wouldn't help. Your family have done a lot for Aslakvaas and its people," said Heinrich.
"If they agree to help us will you be willing to stand with us?" said Anzo.
Heinrich clapped his hands on Anzo's shoulders.

"My friend, you don't even need to ask. We are family now. I will stand with you against the gods if need be," he said.

"Thank you, my friend," said Anzo.

They both smiled and then Heinrich put his arm around Anzo's shoulders.

"Come to the house. We have plenty of food and you have all travelled a long way. Let our joined families eat and drink together," said Heinrich.

They all went into the house. Runo was tending to rabbits and fish that roasted over the fire in the centre of the room. Una walked in from the stable with a bladder of mead and beckoned to them towards the hearth.

"Please find a place to sit. You must be tired from your travels," she said.

They all sat on the furs and skins that lined the floor and passed around the mead.

"I too will stand with you too. No matter what they decide," said Runo.

Anzo and Ruhsarr both nodded and smiled at him.

"Thank you. Your help is welcomed," said Ruhsarr.

"My dad told me if you are going to face a dragon you should take furs with you. You soak them in the river water and when the dragon breathes its fire at you it won't catch alight," said Una.

"Thank you, we'll keep that in mind," said Anzo.

The meat was cut into portions, and each person was handed a piece. As they ate and drank they talked of the predicaments they faced and the possible outcome of the Elder's decision. The food, mead, and conversation made the time pass with ease and soon the light was fading as dusk approached.

"The light is fading. We should go now," said Ruhsarr as he stood up.

"No, we won't make it back before dark," said Anzo.

"But what about the farm?" said Ruhsarr.

"The farm will be fine. I have given them enough reason to stay away," said Anzo.

"Who's staying away?" said Theda.

"We would be grateful if you would allow us to stay here for the night," said Anzo.

"Yes, of course. We're not going to send you out into the night with those things," said Heinrich.

"What things?" said Theda.

"Thank you. You have saved us from having to fight our way home," said Anzo.

"Fighting who?" said Theda.

Ruhsarr gave her a stern look before he spoke.

"There is a Gang of goblin men living around a mile from our farm," he said in a voice just above a whisper.

"Goblin men!" scoffed Theda.

"No, don't speak their name too loud. Some people think that the mere mention of them attracts them closer," said Ruhsarr.

"Really?" said Theda.

"Yes, really," said Ruhsarr.

"The clan of Shrak used to live along the path between our two farms. My grandad and some of the other townsfolk drove them away but they have been trying to settle on this land for a long time. They only usually come out at night and use their strength and the cover of night to attack. They make travelling at night too dangerous to risk. In recent years they have grown brave. I have seen one standing on the tree line in broad daylight. Tall and heavily built. I shot an arrow over his head, and he ran back into the forest a short distance but not as far as I would have liked. I think he is the Ullheem, their leader," said Anzo.

"You should definitely stay here for the night then," said Theda to Ruhsarr. "'We can go back at first light."
He looked down at her and saw the fear in her eyes.

"Ok. Thank you Heinrich and Una. We'll stay here for tonight." he said.
They talked into the night and sang old songs to celebrate the union of their two families.

Anzo opened his eyes at the sounds of birds singing. He sat up and looked around. Everyone around him was still asleep. He had fallen asleep next to the fire. It had died down to little more than embers. He placed some kindling on the ashes and poked at it with a stick. As the kindling began to smoulder he placed a few dried branches on top. As the fire came back to life he got up and brushed the hair from his face. He shook Ruhsarr awake. He then woke Heinrich and soon they were all awake. They broke up two loaves and passed around some apples.

When they had eaten, Anzo and Ruhsarr got ready to travel. As Anzo retrieved Yannee from the stable Theda came out of the home dressed in furs. Ruhsarr put his arm around her and kissed her.

"I will come back for you once I know all this is over," he said.

"I think not. My place is by your side," she said.

"My home is no longer safe. I don't want you to be in danger," he said.

"I don't want you to be in danger either. So does that mean I shouldn't let you go?" she said and gave him a stern look.

"No, I just…" he said.

"Well, that settles it. I'm coming with you," she said and walked past him and helped Anzo ready Yannee for the journey.

Chapter 9.

As they walked along the path to their home they noticed some tracks through the long grass out of the forest. They got closer and saw that the stable door was ajar. Anzo and Ruhsarr drew their axes from their waistbands and ran towards the house. Anzo stopped outside the door and put his hand out to stop Ruhsarr rushing in, in a rage.

"Ok, I'll pull open the door then we go in slow and quiet," he said.

"Ok, I'm ready," said Ruhsarr.

Anzo pulled the door open, and they snuck into the building. There were footprints in the dirt similar to a human foot but with only three toes. They had run all around the stable knocking off tools and equipment. The two men searched the entire building.

"Look, there," said Anzo pointing.

Ruhsarr followed Anzo's finger and looked at what he was pointing at. There in the pen stood a single goat with blood splattered on its flank. It had its face turned as far away from the two men as it possibly could.

"Where's Stosy?" said Ruhsarr.

"This is the work of the goblin men. They must have taken him. They are becoming braver than I thought. They wouldn't have come even close if they had known we were here. Let's search the rest of the house. Make sure none of them have decided to stay for the night," said Anzo.

After twenty minutes they had searched the entire building and found nothing else amiss. They prepared some lunch and sat down to eat.

"What do we do now," said Theda.

"They are long gone. There is no point going to hunt them down. Stosy is probably already eaten. We'll stay up late tonight. If they come back we'll cut them down where they stand," said Ruhsarr.

"He's right. All we can do is wait. In the meantime, those fields aren't going to work themselves," said Anzo. "Come on, son. We have work to do."

They both walked out of the house and took their tools into the field.

"What can I do?" said Theda.

"We have vegetables that are ready for pulling up if you want to do that," said Anzo.

"Consider it done," said Theda.

"Very well," said Anzo and smiled.

The day passed quickly, and the work was going well. Ruhsarr was turning over the soil and planting seeds. He stood up straight and wiped away the sweat that collected on his brow. Theda approached him with a bucket of water and a bowl. She smiled sweetly at him as she dipped the bowl into the bucket and passed it to him. He took it from her with a smile and lifted it to his mouth. As he tipped his head back and drank he looked to the sky. High above him the air was filled with birds all flying in the same direction. He looked back to Theda with a look of fear in his eyes.

"What?" she said with a look of concern on her face.

"It's here," he whispered and looked across the field.

Anzo stood up and looked over to them as a shadow passed over the field he was working in. It was headed in his direction. He waved to them and gestured that he needed a drink.

"Dragon!" shouted Ruhsarr.

Anzo looked up and didn't even have time to flinch. The dragon came down fast and closed its hind feet around him. They pushed deep into the overturned soil as they closed on his body. Anzo tried to scream but the talons of the beast sank deep into his flesh. His bones broke and ruptured his internal organs. No more screams came from him. One final hiss of air was squeezed from his lungs along with a plume of vaporised blood that was ejected from his mouth.

"No!" screamed Ruhsarr.

Theda fell to her knees in shock. The dragon turned its long narrow head to look at them and let out a long hiss. Ruhsarr could have sworn it sounded like laughter. It then flapped its wings downward and rose back into the air. As it flew over the field the last sound Anzo heard was the screams of his son and daughter-in-law.

"No! Father!" scream Ruhsarr as he ran across the field. "Come back you fucking monster. Bring my father back and face me!"

In his heart he knew it was useless, but he kept running until he reached the treeline. There he fell to his knees and there he screamed and sobbed. Theda ran up and fell down next to him. She gathered him up in her arms and held him as he sobbed against her chest.

After a few minutes Ruhsarr rose to his feet. He took Theda's hand in his and with a newfound energy and determination he marched across the field back towards the house. Theda almost had to run to keep up with her husband.

"Where are we going?" said Theda.

"To see the Elders. They will help us now or I will put a mob together myself," he said.

He entered the stable and emerged a few minutes later with Yannee ready to travel. He climbed onto the horse's back and held out his hand. Theda took it and he pulled her up with a strength she had not felt him use on her before. She threw her leg over the horse and held on tight to Ruhsarr's waist.

"Yaarrh!" he roared, and the horse set off at near full gallop away along the forest path.

They reached Aslakvaas faster than they ever had before.

"Open the gates!" roared Ruhsarr as they approached.

"What do you want," said the gatekeeper.

"I need to speak with the Elders, right now!" said Ruhsarr.

"The elders are busy. Come back later," said the gatekeeper.

The rage within Ruhsarr threatened to break free through his chest.

"My father has just been taken by the dragon. You will let me in right now or, by the gods, I will break down these gates with my bare hands," Roared Ruhsarr.

He turned Yannee around and the huge horse reared up then thumped front hooves down against the ground in a show of strength.

The gatekeeper slid the bolt aside and heaved gates wide open. The horse and his two riders thundered into the village and up to the Elder's Hall. Once there he and Theda dismounted and attached Yannee to the horse feeder. They strode over to the door and knocked on the metal plate. There was no answer. Ruhsarr pushed against the doors. They moved a little, so he threw his weight against them and forced them open. He rushed into the building and ran towards the table where the Elders had been sat earlier that day before.

"Where are you? Where are you?" he roared.

Four men each armed with axes stepped from the doorway behind the table. Ruhsarr stopped and backed up a few steps.

"The Elders are conferring. They will not be disturbed," said the tallest of the guards.

People from the village rushed into the building. They surrounded Ruhsarr and Theda with weapons drawn.

"But we need to speak with them. It's urgent," said Ruhsarr.

"I do not care," said the guard. "Leave this place or you will be removed."

The guards and the town's people began to move in on them.

"Tuek, help us!" cried Theda.

The crowd moved closer.

"Tuek!" cried both Theda and Ruhsarr.

There was a movement at the back of the crowd.

"Let me through. Let me through!" said Tuek.

The crowd parted and the old man approached them.

"Ruhsarr, Theda. We told you that we would need a few days to consider your proposal. What is the meaning of all this?" he said with a disapproving expression.

"The dragon, it attacked my father. He's dead, Anzo is dead!" said Ruhsarr.

"Oh, my boy. This is terrible," said Tuek.

"We have to assemble the group of warriors as soon as we can," said Ruhsarr.

"I have some warriors in mind. We will send out word immediately. We will have this dragon moved off your land soon enough," said Tuek.

"I no longer want to move it along. I want to kill it," said Ruhsarr.

Chapter 10.

Tuek and the other Elders called a town meeting. Soon the entire population of Aslakvaas was gathered in the town square. The mid-afternoon summer sun warmed their faces but there was a heavy atmosphere among the crowd. Word had spread fast, and everyone knew about the dragon. The people talked among themselves. There was talk of the beast and where it had been seen. Some stated that the land should be abandoned, while others were spoiling for a fight.

Tuek as the head Elder acted as the speaker for the town. He stepped forwards and addressed the people who numbered just over one hundred. Some of them knew Ruhsarr and Theda or at least knew their parents.

"Good people of Aslakvaas, you have been gathered today because we have a problem. I know that news spreads fast, and with Ruhsarr and Theda's hasty entry through the town gates earlier, I know that you will all by now know the nature of that problem. A dragon has taken residence in the forest of Miehyelzah farm. Earlier today it killed Anzo Miehyelzah and carried him away."

A gasp rose from the crowd and the people began to chatter. Tuek raised his hands to quiet the crowd.

"The threat this beast presents is too high to just allow it to remain where it is. Something has to be done about it and that is why we have gathered you all here. We are asking for volunteers to join a group to hunt this dragon," he said.

A voice rung out from the crowd and interrupted Tuek.

"If it's on the Miehyelzah's land let them deal with it."

Ruhsarr stepped forward towards the crowd.

"My mother died two summers ago, and now my father is dead too. There is no way I could deal with a monster like this by myself. The dragon would be using my ribs to pick its teeth while the sun was still high in the sky. Please, if I didn't need your help would I be asking?" he said.

The people chattered in agreement. Tuek placed his hand on Ruhsarr's shoulder and nodded in approval.

"I know you all have families and land to take care of, but if we leave a threat this great just outside our gates no one is safe. Not a single one of us. That is why we are looking for volunteers to step forwards and help, not only Ruhsarr and Theda, but all of us," said Tuek.

"But fighting a dragon is certain death," someone shouted.

Some of the members of the crowd cheered their agreed.

"Death? We will all know death at some time in our lives. Death will come to each and every one of us. The question we should ask ourselves is how we want to meet our ancestors in that valley of the gods. On our feet, or on our knees!?" said Tuek.

The crowd roared and began to rile themselves up with chants.

"Dragons can be killed. I have seen it! We need warriors. Who wants to be remembered in the songs of heroes?!" called Tuek.

The crowd reached fever pitch and the bravest among them began to step forwards. Soon there was a line of people forming at the front of the crowd. Ruhsarr looked at them all and the emotion within him began to change from sadness into pride. These people were willing to step up to the challenge of defending their land. The frown he wore began to ease into something resembling a smile.

Tuek held up his hands.

"People of Aslakvaas. We have our warriors. You are the bravest of us all. Your actions will determine the future of our town, and this land. Before us stand Brolm Huetel, Rowben Stonehall, Iteck Jass, Hummie Lioto, Jagga Rivejer, Goto Himmerswear, Umber Troolu, Droober Dullin, Hateish Ragmar, and Yuli Simmehan. We thank you for what you are about to do for the good of us all," he said.

"Thank you for offering to stand beside me in my time of greatest need. This will not be an easy task, but I know with your strength and courage we will be victorious," said Ruhsarr.

"We do this for you, for the people of Aslakvaas, and for honour," said Brolm as he clapped his hand down on Ruhsarr's shoulder.

"The dragon with be ferocious but he will fall before us," said Hummie as she raised her axe above her head.

"By the time the sun kisses the distant hills tomorrow the dragon's skull will be our trophy," said Goto.

"Are we going to stand about kissing each other's arses all day or are we going to go and kill a fucking dragon?" said Hateish and knocked his two battle axes together.

"First we all eat, drink, and give our praise to the gods of the valley," said Tuek.

The people cheered sang and knocked their axe heads together. A meal was prepared for the warriors, Ruhsarr and Theda in the Elder's Hall. The people of the town ate alongside them. Bladders filled with mead were passed around. Songs were chanted to the gods of iron for the weapons to be strong and sharp. To the gods of the land and the skies for fair weather and clear paths. To the gods of flesh for strength, speed of limbs, for courage, and a steady mind in the fight that would soon take place.

Also a song was sung to all the gods for a safe return, or good death. When the prayers were completed Tuek stood and raised his hands.

"Kiss your families. For some this may be the last time you hold each other near in this life. We know, no matter what fate now has in store for you, you will bring great honour on our people and our land. The time has come for you to walk beyond the walls of this town and into the unpredictable seas of battle. May you all return safely. Gods go with you." he said.

"Gods go with you!" all the people gathered in the great hall chanted.

The warriors embraced their families. There were tears and smiles and kisses. The warriors then took up their weapons and packs and began the journey to Ruhsarr's home.

Chapter 11.

Upon their arrival Ruhsarr put Yannee in the stable. The Warriors stood outside the house and looked out across the fields towards the forest and the hills that peeked out over the tree canopy. As Ruhsarr stepped out from the stable to join them.

"Which hill is the dragon trying to take for its home?" said Goto.

"The tallest closest one with the rock formations towards its summit," said Ruhsarr.

"I was expecting a longer distance to walk. I see now why it is a problem we all share," said Goto.

"It's only a short journey, but it's the greatest journey we'll ever make. The people of this land are counting on us to rid them of this threat," said Ruhsarr.

"And so we shall, but first we must sleep. Tomorrow is a new day, and it starts with a hike through Goblin infested forest. Our senses must be as sharp as the blades we carry," said Hateish.

"Goblins?" said Goto.

"There are goblins, but they keep their distance, and it's not exactly and infestation," said Ruhsarr.

"Aye, but if we do come across any they will be half the goblin they once were. Did I ever tell you about the time I sliced one of the cunts down the middle; from the top of the head to the sack of his balls?" said Hateish.

"No, but that is a story I want to hear. Come in. The fire is warm, and the bedding is comfortable. Tales of victory, and then rest are a must this night," said Theda as she beckoned them all inside.

"At first light we head into the forest and take back our land," said Ruhsarr

The group of men and women happily made their way into the house. There they bedded down and told their stories until sleep visited them all.

Chapter 12.

Just before the sun rose Ruhsarr woke up. He sat up and pulled his furs around him. Theda groaned and stretched next to him. He smiled down at her and kissed her mouth.

"Good morning," he said.

"Good morning," she said with a smile.

"We better wake these lot up. You have a long day ahead of us," she said.

"I've got just the thing," he said as he leaned over and stoked the fire.

He skewered some salted mutton and hung it over the fire. The smell of the cooking meat drifted through the room gently waking the warriors.

"That smells amazing," said Droober.

"Yeah, my mouth was watering before my eyes were open," said Jagga and smiled.

As they all got up Ruhsarr handed them chunks of meat and bread. Soon they had all eaten and were getting dressed and equipped for what lay ahead of them. Axes and spears were sharpened, bows strings were tightened, and arrows were checked. Dew still clung to the grass as they made their way out into the field. An early morning mist was quickly evaporating as the sun rose over the horizon. Two men appeared on the path walking towards the house.

"Do you know these men?" said Goto.

"Dad, Runo!" said Theda and ran to them. "I was beginning to think you weren't coming."

"That thing killed Anzo. He was family. I want to see that dragon dead as much as Ruhsarr," said Heinrich.

Ruhsarr nodded and place his hand on his father in laws shoulder and pulled him into a hug.

“You are the closest thing I have to a father now. It’s an honour to be part of your family,” said Ruhsarr and fought back tears and released his grip.

“The honour is ours,” said Heinrich.

Ruhsarr then grabbed Runo and hugged him too.

“We are here for you, brother. Come whatever may,” said Runo.

They all stood and looked around at each other for a moment. Then Ruhsarr opened his mouth and bellowed.

“Warriors, are we ready to face this day?! Are we ready to fight?!”

They all raised their weapons high and roared.

“Then let us hunt a fucking dragon,” he said.

The warriors beat their weapons upon their shields. Ruhsarr led the pack from the front as they walked across the fields towards the treeline.

The forest was dense, and the undergrowth completely obscured the ground in some places. They followed a sparsely trodden path that Anzo and Ruhsarr took whenever they travelled this way. As they moved among the tree they could feel the eyes of non-human being watching their every move. Birds called out and flapped their wings as they were startled from their roosting places. Unseen things moved the foliage and scurried away from this hunting party. As the warriors walked they communicated with hand gestures and facial expressions. There were other predators in this forest beside the one that they hunted. They were watched from afar by a tall dark green skinned Goblin man. He however, made no move to close the distance between them.

Sooner than some of them would have liked, they arrived at the foot of the hill. Ruhsarr looked back and saw their follower. He and the goblin man locked eyes. It shook its head and frowned to signify what it thought of their intentions, then ducked down and silently slipped back into the thick foliage. The party stopped at the treeline and looked up the hill. Smoke rose from smouldering fires in the surrounding area of the cave. The warriors crouched down and moved into the undergrowth.

"How are we going to approach the beast?" said Jagga.

Ruhsarr looked at him and then looked up the hill. He spoke slowly and thoughtfully so the group could hear.

"We're downwind of it so it doesn't yet know we are here. That is assuming at hunts by scent. We already know it definitely hunts by sight. It may also have other senses that we don't understand. So, I'm thinking we should spread out then approach slowly and quietly on three sides. A small group can then enter the cave and flush the dragon out. As it exits the cave those of us outside will move in and overwhelm it with a simultaneous attack before it can retaliate. It is us who will be the heroes by days end," said Ruhsarr.

"My wife promised to ride me like a stallion if I return so I intend to turn this beast into nothing more than cuts of meat and bones," said Hateish. They all smiled at this and held in their laughter.

"It's a good a reason as any," said Ruhsarr. "Let's spread out. On my signal we move. Understood?" Each one of them nodded.

They spread out around the foot of the hill all making sure to keep in cover. As they ascended the hill they reached a height where they could see the Miehyelzah farm. Aslakvaas was a structure in the distance. When they were all in position Ruhsarr looked from Jagga to his left and then to Iteck on his right. He nodded to them, and they nodded to the warrior next on from them. They all began to steadily climb up the hill, quickly moving from one point of cover to the next. Soon they were all closing in on the mouth of the cave but advancing from different angles. Outside the cave the roasted and partially eaten remains of a bovine animal smouldered in the morning air. Its bones jutting out at odd angles like the fingers of a broken hand. Jagga quietly stepped past it and approached the dark gaping void in the hilltop. She stopped just to one side the cave and listened. Ruhsarr and Iteck moved in then all three of them slipped into the darkness.

Inside their eyes adjusted to the low light. As they moved forwards the only sound they heard was the dripping of water onto stone. The deeper they went the more they could hear the low whistle of huge lungs drawing in and exhaling air. A few moments later they could make out the shape of the beast curled up at the far end of the cave. The smell of burnt and rotting flesh filled the air. Iteck retched quietly but managed to keep his breakfast down. Ruhsarr gave him a stern look. Iteck signalled that he was ok, and Ruhsarr looked back to the dragon. Jagga drew her battle axe and silently made her approach. Iteck drew an arrow from his quill and readied it on his bow. As he drew it back the string creaked. The dragon's eyes opened ever so slightly. Seeing the warrior approach the eyes snapped fully open and the inner eyelids slid aside. Jagga raised her axe and stepped forwards at the same time that Iteck loosed the arrow. The dragon lunged forwards and snapped its jaws tight around Jagga's waist. Its serrated teeth cut deep into her flesh, and she let out a scream. The arrow buried itself in the dragon's shoulder, but it didn't seem to bother the beast in the slightest.

It thrashed its head on the end of its long muscular neck with such force that Jagga was shaken like a rag doll. The force caused her flesh to tear, and its long teeth sliced deeper into her body. Her hips and legs were hurled in one direction while the top half of her torso was sent in another. Blood and viscera were scattered in all directions. The dragon chomped on the morsel of warrior that remained in its mouth then swallowed. Iteck quickly drew and readied another arrow then released it, but the dragon was already running directly at him. He turned and ran but just as he made it to the mouth of the cave a huge burst of flames flared out all around him. The warriors outside watched as he became a silhouette in the dragon's flames. The fire consumed him, and he screamed as he threshed. He fell to his knees as the flesh melted from his bones. The dragon charged out from the mouth of the cave, smashing through the remains of Iteck, scattering body parts, and throwing them down the hill. The other warriors fled down the hill. While some found hiding places others ran down into the forest and didn't look back.

Still inside the cave Ruhsarr crouched in the darkness, biting the edge of his furs to keep from screaming. The dragon galloped down the hill and grabbed Brolm. It held him up in its hands. The man screamed and thrashed wildly until the dragon took his head in its mouth. Its teeth sliced into his neck. With a swift movement it took off his head. Blood gushed from the base of his neck as the dragon cast his body aside and moved on. It snorted the air as it went, crashing through the stump of a dead tree. Runo and Umber on the other side of it were thrown bloodied and broken from their hiding place. It pinned Umber to the ground with its hand in the centre of his back. It bit into his neck and tore the flesh and bones from his shoulders and neck with bird-like movements. Four arrows hit it all from different directions, but they only angered the beast even more. Goto ran silently from his hiding place and swung both his axes, burying one into its left shoulder and the other into its ribs. The beast reared up and batted him away with its hand. He was thrown from the hillside with entrails unravelling from his split open abdomen before he crashed through the canopy of the forest. More arrows struck the beast, but it strode around unaffected. Ruhsarr ran to the mouth of the cave and watched as Rowben slipped out from her hiding place and into another behind a bush. The beast turned and snorted the air as it strode in her direction. Ruhsarr watched as the woman sunk down further into her hiding place. The Beast breathed out a burst of flame that engulfed the entire bush, Rowben and everything in its proximity. She screamed as her flesh seared and melted. The Dragon then strode over and forced its head through the brush and picked up Rowben's still writhing body in its jaws. Her flesh crunched as its teeth sliced into her body. It withdrew its head and swallowed huge chunks for her. Ruhsarr took a deep breath, crouched down and ran out from the cave and hid with Hummie behind a boulder. They peeked out from either side of their hiding place. They watched as the dragon approached Runo who still lay injured on the hillside. Hummie then drew an arrow from his quiver and readied it on his bow. He stood up and loosed the arrow at the dragon. It hit and buried itself in the right side of the beast's snout. It turned and shot a long narrow ark of flame directly at Hummie. He was instantly engulfed in flames and fell to the ground. He croaked as the flames seared his throat. Moments later he was dead. Ruhsarr peeked over the boulder and saw that the dragon was approaching him. He flattened himself against the boulder and waited as his heart pounded in his chest. There was nowhere to go. If he moved the dragon would see him. He steadied his nerves and readied his battle axe. A few seconds later the dragon's snout appeared around the side of the boulder and snorted at Hummie's body. Ruhsarr held his breath as the beast nudged the body with its snout. He realised that the dragon didn't know he was there. Without hesitation he swung the axe up over his head stepped forwards and brought it down. The dragon's eye saw the glint of the sunlight on the blade, but it was already too late. The axe crashed into its head just behind its right eye and sunk deep into its skull. It reared up on to its back legs and took Ruhsarr with it. He wrapped his legs and one arm around its neck and drew out his long knife. As he repeatedly plunged the blade into the beast's muscular neck, Hateish ran from his hiding place brandishing his axes. He swung one hard into the dragon's right ankle and another into its knee. He pulled the axe from the ankle smashed it into the hip of the beast. This happened in quick succession with devastating effect. The axes split its scales, sliced the flesh and cleaved the bones beneath. As the dragon fell onto its side Heinrich ran in and thrust his spear into the dragon's chest, piercing its heart. He wrenched the spear from side to side and cut the organ in half. Blood gushed out from the wound. Ruhsarr stood pulled his axe from the dragon's head, raise the weapon up and brought it down through its neck, separating the head. The body writhed and shuddered for a moment, before falling limp and dead. The three men stood drew and heaving breaths.

"It's, it's done," panted Ruhsarr.

All three men then knelt down and Ruhsarr spoke.

"As our fathers have done before us and as our children will when we are gone, we thank you. Thank you for your speed, for your strength, your eyes, your ears, your nose, and your fire. We hope you will gift us with these things as you have gifted your flesh and your skins so we may live. You have been a mighty warrior and a worthy opponent. May you run free in the hallowed forests of the next life," he said.

The three men then worked together to skin the scales and hide from the dragon's body. They cut as much meat away as they could. They took its claws and the leather of its wings. All this they piled onto sleighs they made from the trunks of small trees. They collected the bodies and remains of the party together and buried them next to each other on the summit of the hill. They helped Runo to his feet and were relieved that he was able to walk. However, both his arms were broken. Heinrich helped him cross them over his chest while Ruhsarr bound long strips of material around his body to hold the limbs in place. They all then made their way down the hill into the forest. As they walked every living thing that surrounded them was still and silent.

Chapter 13.

Theda saw them as they stepped out from the treeline of the forest and crossed the fields towards the farm. She was stood at the door waiting and dropped the cup she held in her hands. She ran to them as Runo's weary legs began to give way.

"By the Gods, am I glad to see you," she said as she caught him.

"The Gods smiled on us this day," said Heinrich.

"Is it done? Is the dragon dead?" she said.

"It's done," said Ruhsarr as he patted the dragon's head that sat on top of his sleigh.

Its jaw swung loose, and its long tongue lulled out over its teeth.

"That is a wonderful, but somewhat disgusting sight," said Theda.

"I'm going to hang it above the door to keep the Goblins away," Ruhsarr said with a smile.

Theda laughed.

"We need to go and see the Elders and Runo needs to see a healer. We must also inform them of the lives the dragon took. It killed seven of us. Three ran after seeing it burn Iteck alive," said Ruhsarr.

The four men looked at their feet solemnly.

"Let's get Yannee. Runo, you can ride him. You don't look too good," said Theda.

With some effort Runo managed to nod.

"First we should eat and drink," said Heinrich.

They all agreed. When they had all eaten and Heinrich helped Runo onto the horse, they set off back towards Aslakvaas.

It was the late afternoon by the time they reached the walled town. As they approached the gates creaked and groaned as they swung open. The weary group trudged through the streets towards the hill upon which the Elders Hall stood. A crowd of people grew around them and followed, anxious to know the results of the expedition and to know what had happened to their family members. They were halfway up the hill when the doors opened and Tuek and the other Elders stepped out from the building and walked down the hill to greet them.

"We are glad to see you have returned. Does this mean that the dragon is dead," he said.

Ruhsarr nodded.

"It does," he said.

"You say the dragon is dead, so where are our people?" said a person in the crowd.

"Where is Jagga?" said a man.

"Where is my Goto?" said a woman.

"They fought well but the beast was the strongest and most ferocious animal I have ever encountered in my life," said Ruhsarr.

"Our warriors are dead?" said another person.

"We all knew the risks of sending our people to face a dragon. You heard Ruhsarr. The dragon is dead, so let him speak," said Tuek.

"The dragon was the most aggressive and intelligent animal I have ever pitted myself against. Its strength was unmatched. It moved with the savagery of a bear and the elegance of an eagle, all while spouted fire from its mouth. We four making it out alive is purely down to an attack of brute strength. Our arrows were of no hindrance to its thick skin. We had to get in close and hit it with axes and spears in a united attack," said Ruhsarr.

"We all risked our lives today. We risked them for you," said Hateish.

"Umber and Droober returned earlier. Both are still wild with fear and babbling about the beast and its ability to spit flames. Yuli has not yet returned," said Tuek.

"They fled when the dragon burned Iteck. I'm surprised they were the only three," said Ruhsarr. A woman in the crowd cried out in anguish.

"You have robbed us of our family members!" she shouted.

Tuek threw up his hands and the crowd settled a little.

"It is not Ruhsarr who has robbed you. It was the dragon and the dragon alone. Remember that Ruhsarr has also lost his father to this beast. If he had not asked for our help it would have only been a matter of time before it attacked our town. We are not equipped to defend ourselves against a creature that can take to the air and spit fire. We would have all perished to the might of the beast. Our fighters showed bravery in the face of adversity. In giving their lives they have defended ours. These men stood before you risked their lives to defend us, all of us. They deserve our gratitude, not condemnation," he said.

The crowd bowed their heads.

"I am sorry for the loss of our people. I wish all of them could have returned with us. We have all lost in this battle, but we need to pull together now more than ever. If ever a dragon returns to our lands we need to be ready. We need to make weapons and train to fight for all we have. If not we will lose what we have built here. We will lose what your fighters gave their lives for," said Ruhsarr.

"I don't believe there was a dragon. I think you just made it up. You just want fame and glory," said a man in the crowd.

In reply Ruhsarr swung a large bundle from his back. He untied the twine holding it closed, reached in and took hold of one of the spines. He pulled the fabric away and held aloft the dragon's head. Its scales reflected the late afternoon sun, and the crowd swooned.

"The dragon was real. You who say otherwise, you can argue with the blood that coats my axes," said Hateish.

The man stepped back and scampered away.

"This is a time for celebration of our warriors both standing and fallen," said Tuek.

The crowd began to sing for Ruhsarr and the dragon slayers.

"Come, tell us of their bravery. So that we can remember them in our songs," said one of women.

Tuek led the remaining warriors and the town's people into the Elders Hall. They listened to Ruhsarr and the others as they recounted the bravery of the warriors. How they had stood against the dragon and eventually slain the beast.

Chapter 14.

Ruhsarr and Theda returned home to their farmland. Ruhsarr looked across the field to the place where he had last seen his father. He looked to the treeline of the forest, then over the trees to the hill. The place where all those good people had lost their lives to a dragon. The bones of that dragon still lay where it had fallen, along with the graves of those brave fallen warriors. He felt a sense of guilt over how those people had lost their lives, yet he was one of the survivors. He reminded himself of Tuek words. They gave their lives to save everyone else. His thoughts settled for a moment. A pang of sadness rose in his chest then and tears welled in his eyes. As a child this place had a sense of magic and wonder. His father, the intelligent farmer and bold warrior had held a god-like status in Ruhsarr's mind. And his mother had been a figure of strength and knowledge to him. She had known the forest like the back of her hand. The plants and trees held no secrets from her. They had both moulded Ruhsarr into the man he was today, but now they were both gone. He lifted his hand to his face and wept. He remembered the things they had taught him, and the lessons he had learnt. He could almost hear Anzo speaking to as if he was still here. His mother's voice, despite his best efforts to hold on to it, was fading from his memory. A hand rested on his shoulder. He turned to see Theda's sad smile. He tried to turn away, but she pulled him into a hug.

"There is no need to be ashamed of crying. You have been through a lot over the past few days. You are allowed to cry," she said.

"I just can't believe that they are both gone. I keep expecting dad to still be here when I get back, but

then I remember that he's gone. There isn't even a body to bury," he said.
Theda rubbed his back and held him.
"I am sure they are together now. The gods know where to find us when we die. His body has returned to the earth, and he will walk with your ancestors now," she said.
He nodded and the tears that streamed down his face calved paths through the grime and ash that coated his skin. She kissed him and her lips were warm and tender against his.
"Her voice is fading from my mind. I remember all the words she spoke to me, yet the sound of them is slipping away," he said.
"Come on, my dear. You are tired and upset. Sleep will do you good. Come on," she said.
She led him by the hand, and he followed without resistance. He had lost so much but still had her. He knew now that she was a tower of strength for him when he felt so fragile and vulnerable. She made him realise that his tears were not a sign of weakness but an after effect of the strength he had already displayed. She could have run back to her parents and abandoned him when the dragon had tried to claim his land, but she stuck with him. She was as strong as him in her own way. They were equals and allies in life. He loved her before but now he knew he loved her with his soul as well as his body. A small smile crept onto his face as she led him into their home. He felt the gods smile upon them and he knew life would get better for them.

Chapter 15.

As the year progressed the two of them dried and smoked meats and baked hard breads to survive the winter months. They continued to hunt animals and trade the meat, furs and bones with the people of the surrounding towns. As the spring approached they fell back into the routine of maintaining the farm. They grew crops and reared animals to trade with the people of Aslakvaas. Whenever they ventured into the town the people greeted them. They had been dubbed 'the mighty dragon slayers: Saviours of Aslakvaas.' They were given food and ale as offerings but always gave the people something in return.

One morning Ruhsarr and Theda stepped out into the fields to pick the crops and feed the animals. They heard the noise of feet walking and the chatter of an approaching group. Instinctively Ruhsarr and Theda immediately had their hands on their axes, ready for whatever rounded the corner and approached them from the path. A Group of people they recognised from the Town walked towards them from the area of the path obscured by the trees.

"Good morning. Is everything well in the town?" said Theda.

"Yes, lady Theda. We are here to help you. You have done so much for us we have decided to help you tend to your land," said the man who led the group.

"Thank you, but we are doing well," said Ruhsarr.

"Many hands are better than four. The end of summer will approach faster than anyone expects. We want to help you in your work before the cold seasons come again," said a woman.

Ruhsarr looked at Theda and she smiled at him.

“Very well. You are all welcome to help us. We can only offer you food in return though,” he said.

“That is all we require. It will be an honour to work for the slayers of the dragon,” said the man. Ruhsarr was about to say something along the lines of: “You don’t have to call us that.” But he had learned that the people insisted on this title, so he simply smiled and nodded.

Soon they had a workforce of around twenty people turning up every morning to work.
They were able to cut a new field from the land and grew more wheat and barley alongside their leafy greens and beats. They began to bake large amounts of bread and baked goods which they could feed the workers with and use to trade in the town. Life was good and they began to fall into a highly sustainable state.

Hateish was treated the same way in the town. A few times its people had asked him to consider a roll among the Elders, but he always turned down the offer.

“I am a blacksmith first and foremost. A weapons maker, the forger of metals, and the builder of shields. I will stand alongside my people. I have no wish to rule,” he would say.
Despite his humble nature he too benefitted from people wanting to work for a hero. He would forge tools for The Miehyelzah farm and in return he and his family were well fed.

Each new moon he would take a cart full of tools to Ruhsarr and Theda. On this occasion he loaded up something special. Something he had been working on for most of a year. He clicked his tongue, and his horses began to haul the cart out from the space between his house and his forge. Then out beyond the town’s walls and towards The Miehyelzah farm. Soon the farmhouse came into view and both he and the horses breathed a sigh of relief.

Ruhsarr stood in the field and looked in Hateish's direction as he brought his cart to a stop alongside the house. He strolled through the field patting the occasional farmhand on the shoulder and speaking words of encouragement. As he approached Hateish the two of them looked at each other and smiled.

"It's good to see you, my friend," said Ruhsarr.

"And you. I'll never get tired of seeing that handsome face. Look at that jaw, like it was chiselled from the finest marble," said Hateish.

"You say the kindest thing, but I know your heart is really filled with your namesake," said Ruhsarr. Theda had walked over by this time and Hateish looked at her.

"You hear the way your husband talks to me? Wounded! Wounded I am. Cover your ears, Theda. A woman should not be witness to such vile hostility!" said Hateish.

Ruhsarr and Theda laughed. Then Hateish gathered them both up in a hug.

"What have you brought for us today?" said Ruhsarr when Hateish had finally let him go.

"I have the finest tools in all the land. Blades and spades, knives and scythes. But first I want to show you something that I have been working on since we arrived back in Aslakvaas on that fateful day," said Hateish.

"I'm intrigued," said Ruhsarr.

"Oh, you should be. This is a thing of pure and unrivalled beauty," said Hateish.

He lifted the item from the cart. It was a large shield covered in a cloth sheet. He slid his arm into the strap on the back and gripped the handle. Then, as he held it out in front of himself, he made a grandiose sweeping gesture towards the shield. It was rectangular in shape and about two thirds of Ruhsarr's height.

"Observed the size. You can kneel behind it and be completely obscured," said Hateish.

"This is impressive. I've never seen a shield this large. But why is it covered with the sheet?" said Ruhsarr.

"Ah," said Hateish holding up his index finger. He grabbed the sheet and whipped it away. The outer surface had been expertly wrapped in the scale covered skin of the dragon.

Ruhsarr and Theda's jaws dropped.

"This is amazing," said Ruhsarr.

"Aye, she is, and she belongs to you," said Hateish.

"That is very kind, but I can't just take your wares off you. I must give you something in return," said Ruhsarr.

"It is a gift. From one dragon slayer to another," said Hateish.

"But, what if you need it. You should keep it," said Ruhsarr.

"I have already run my extremely adept brain over that matter, and that's the reason I made four. This one belongs to you. You are welcome," said Hateish with a smug smile.

"This is incredible. Thank you, so much. What a beautiful gift," said Ruhsarr.

"Not only is she pretty, she is also functional. The scales add to the strength of the underlying oak and iron form. No axe will break this shield. It is also completely fireproof. If one day one of those scaly mother fuckers dares even look at our lands we will be ready," said Hateish.

Ruhsarr looked at him and nodded.

Chapter 16.

The months ebbed away, and a cold winter came and passed. As the ice and snow on the mountains melted the rivers ran thick with fresh melt water. The birds sang and the animals of the forests began their breeding seasons.

Ruhsarr walked through the forest and along the river. He was heading for the fishing spot his family had used for generations. There was a spring in his step as he thought about all the lovely fish he would be bringing home for his wife and their friends. He fought his way through the undergrowth and cut a path through the overgrown brush. Around him he heard the occasional rustle of leaves due to the disturbance of resting wildlife. He got the distinct feeling that someone was keeping up with him but also keeping their distance from him as he moved among the trees. Soon he turned with the river and could almost see the fishing spot. A smile played across his face, but it was short lived.

A large figure stepped onto the path around ten steps ahead of him. The marble-like skin of their arms and legs told him this was no human. The clothes they wore was thick and of a weave like none he had seen so close up before. The pungent scent of Earth and plant matter emanated from this person. They held their head bowed low and long matted hair obscured the face.

"Erm…Good morning to you," said Ruhsarr.

As this person raised their head he saw they had a snout-like face and large, turquoise, almond shaped eyes. This cemented in his mind that this indeed was no human. He hand never seen one of the forest folk so close up. He had imagined that they would be elegant and beautiful. This one was strong built and clearly a seasoned warrior. They cocked their head to the side, parted their lips in a snarl, and squinted their eyes. Ruhsarr could tell that there was nothing good about the morning for this being.

"You and your kind are no longer welcome here," they said slowly in a thick accent unlike any Ruhsarr had heard before.

"Can I ask why not?" said Ruhsarr.

"You have changed things in the land that should not be changed. You have affected the balance of this world," said the being.

"Are you talking about the fields we made? We can leave the land to grow wild again if that would appease you and your kin," said Ruhsarr.

The being growled.

"It is not the fields. Lands change. You took something that cannot be given back. You took one of the few remaining old ones," said the being.

"You are talking about the dragon?" said Ruhsarr.

"The Old ones are border guardians. They protect the fringes of our worlds. To take one does great harm," said the being.

"It was trying to claim my land," said Ruhsarr.

"Foolish Human. These lands do not belong to us or you. We are here to help and grow the fruits of the land. You are a danger. You are no longer allowed to step across the veil into our lands again. You are no longer free to take the fish you have enjoyed," said the being.

Ruhsarr took a step forward and opened his mouth to speak but stopped when the being lifted it hand and waved a finger at him.

"Ah, ah. I have more eyes on you than you would believe. Enough arrows pointed at you that your life could be taken more times than you can understand. The deal your family have benefited from is over. You have broken the bond. All connections between my people and your people are severed. You walk

these lands now on your own. The Fey and Humans are no longer aligned," said the being.
Tears welled in Ruhsarr's eyes.

"I'm sorry. I had no idea we had such a connection. I didn't know killing a dragon carried such consequences," he said.

"Your words are hollow and spoken too late. What is done is done. Now you must leave or suffer," said the being as it turned away from him.
The anger grew in Ruhsarr just as strong as the day Anzo was killed. Before he could stop himself he opened his mouth and began to speak.

"That land belongs to my family and has done for many generations. The dragon killed my father that means the land is now mine. The dragon wanted the land, and I just couldn't allow that. I don't care what you say. The land is mine. It belongs to me," said Ruhsarr.
The being turned and strode towards Ruhsarr. He stepped back but was not fast enough. The being reached out a hand towards his head and gripped him by the hair. At the same time it pulled a long white blade from its waistband. It moved the blade to Ruhsarr's face and pushed it into his mouth. There was a squeak as it slid between his upper and lower incisors.

"The hill is a vail border and the guardians are inevitable. If you ever return here I will butcher you myself and make blades from your bones. I will then use those blades to cut down and butcher every single human your life has affected in any way. Nod if you understand," said the being.
Ruhsarr nodded and whimpered as a hot stream of urine flowed down his legs.

It was around midday when he stepped back into his house. Tired and dejected with only a hen and a hand full of eggs. Theda looked to him and smiled, but when she saw his expression her smile slipped from her face.

"What happened, my love? Where are the fish," she said.

Ruhsarr shook his head and frowned.

"The Forest Folk, they wouldn't let me pass. I'm not allowed to go there anymore," he said.

"What? Why?" she said.

Ruhsarr shrugged.

"They are angry that we killed the dragon. They said that dragons are guardians, that they are inevitable," he said.

Theda looked confused.

"What does that mean?" she said.

"I don't know. I think it means we can't stop the dragons. There will always be more of them," he said.

"I hope not," she said.

"I don't understand though. There has never been a dragon there before in my lifetime. Nor in my father's," he said.

"So, why would they start coming now?" she said.

He shook his head.

"I don't know. I think they might just have been forcing me out. Some of the Forest Folk have never liked that my family had an agreement with some of their families. I have never seen the one from today before. I think they are just using the dragon as an excuse to break the agreement. Telling me there will be more to try and scare us away, but this is my family's land. This is our land now and, dragons or not, we aren't leaving," he said.

"But if there was another, what would we do?" she said.

"I said we are not leaving!" he growled.

Chapter 17.

Six years passed and the town of Aslakvaas grew. It drew people in from across the land to both trade and settle. When new people arrived the town's people would sing them the songs of Ruhsarr, Hateish and the dragon hunters. Through these songs the story of their bravery travelled when these people returned to their own villages and towns. The story of how they killed a dragon quickly became a part of the local folklore. Ruhsarr and Theda's farm grew too. They claimed a large area from the wildlands to breed and rear animals.

Ruhsarr and Theda left the farm in the capable hands of their work force and walked to The Graven Farm. They arrived and Heinrich greeted them with open arms. He led them into the house where Una had a stew cooking on the fire. She ushered them in and had them sit down.

"It's wonderful to see the both of you. You're so busy these days I feel like we barely see you," said Una.

"I know. The farm is getting busier all the time. We have left Myros in charge of the farm," said Theda.

"Ah yes. Myros. She is very knowledgeable when it comes to raising crops," said Heinrich.

"Yes. She's taught us both many things," said Ruhsarr.

"Well, it's wonderful to see you," said Una as she split the meat and vegetables onto five plates.

They ate and talked and laughed about all the things that had happened since their last visit. The conversation turned to the dragon.

"I still dream from time to time that we are still on that hill. It takes me a while to remember that I am home and safe," said Heinrich.

"It is strange how it stays with you. I sometimes hear its roars just as I wake up," said Ruhsarr.

"How is Runo? Do you think he feels the same?" said Theda.

"I have heard him cry out in his sleep in the past. He still has some aches and pains in his arms occasionally," said Una.

At that moment almost on cue Runo stepped into the house. He held a hare in one hand, a pheasant in the other, and a bow was slung over his left shoulder. They all turned to look at him. He looked at them and smiled.

"Were you talking about me?" he said.

"We were talking about how we've all been coping with things since the dragon," said Theda.

"I can do light work in the fields and hunt with a bow. Though my days of hunting anything bigger than these two are gone, and forget me cutting anything with an axe," said Runo.

From outside the house came the sound of galloping horse hooves and a male voice shouting.

"Ruhsarr, Theda!"

The five of them ran out to see Yannee skidding to a halt a few yards from the house. The man on his back was Hark, one of the farm hands.

"Ruhsarr, Theda. You have to come quick. Dolna has vanished," he said.

"What do you mean, vanished?" said Ruhsarr as he furrowed his brow in confusion.

"We were working in the field near the treeline. I turned away from him for one moment and when I looked back he was gone. The trees were moving as if something had disturbed them. There was blood splashed across the crops he had been picking but Dolna was nowhere to be seen," said Hark.

"You think someone took him?" said Theda.

"Yes, I do. He was no further from me than I am from you right now, but I heard nothing. No noise at all. I raised the alarm and Myros sent me to fetch you," said Hark.
Ruhsarr looked at the sky and saw there were still many hours of daylight left.

"Ok, Hark, you go on ahead and tell Myros we are on our way," he said, then turned to Heinrich, Una and Runo. "Sorry but we are going to have to cut this visit short. We'll come again in a few days."

"Don't worry, we understand. Go and see what has happened to your worker," said Heinrich.

They all said their goodbyes and then Ruhsarr and Theda set off on the path home.

By the time they reached their farm the sun was getting low in the sky. They walked up to the house and were greeted by Myros and Hark.

"Good to see you are both safe," said Myros.

"And you. Thank you for sending Hark to bring us home," said Theda.

"I sent all the hands home. I had them searched the surrounding area, but they are scared and nervous. No more good work could be done today," said Myros.

"Good initiative. I wouldn't have wanted them here getting worked up and demanding something be done before I even know what is happening," said Ruhsarr.

"Come this way. We'll show you where he was last seen," said Myros.
They walked across the field until Hark spoke.

"It was here that I last saw him," he said.
A man's stride length away from the treeline stood a line of crops. Some of the fruit had been picked along the line but after a clearly defined point the fruit was still attached to the plants. At this point it

and many of the plants around were splashed and spotted with dark, dried blood. It was clear from the amount that Dolna had sustained a severe and maybe fatal injury. Ruhsarr looked at the scene and then to Hark.

"You heard nothing when the attack happened?" he said.

"That's right. Nothing at all. He was just gone. The blood was the only sign that there had been someone stood here," said Hark.

Ruhsarr knelt down to get a closer look at the area. There were two footprints in the soft soil where Dolna had been stood, then blood and nothing more.

"There are no drag marks from his feet, or signs of a struggle. Whatever took him lifted him off the ground," he said.

"Whatever took him? You don't think it was a person?" said Myros.

"I've seen the damage people do. This looks like an animal attack," he said.

"What do you think it was?" she said.

Ruhsarr looked at the undergrowth beyond the treeline. There was an area that had been pushed aside and trodden down.

"Something big," he said.

He crossed the treeline and walked into the disturbed undergrowth. The others followed him. He inspected the ground there, moving some of the leaves and the soil. After a while Ruhsarr looked up from the ground and out into the forest beyond. He saw the movement of a figure flitting from one tree to another.

"Look there," he said.

"Is that a goblin?" said Myros.

"Yes," said Ruhsarr.

"Do you think they took Dolna?" said Hark

“No, they can be dangerous, but they are not strong enough to take a fully grown man this easily with no signs of a struggle,” said Ruhsarr.

He turned his attention back to the ground. The earth had been disturbed but the markings were not clear enough to be able to tell what had made them. He looked back up to the forest.

“There is nothing more we can do here. You should go home. The sun will be setting in an hour. Tell Dolna's family that we are sorry. We will resume the search in the morning,” he said.

“Ok. I'll see you tomorrow,” said Myros.

She patted Hark on the shoulder and they both walked back through the field towards the house and then back to Aslakvaas.

Ruhsarr and Theda made sure the farm was secure, and all the animals were safe. They turned in for the night, though, neither of them got much sleep. Every sound had them on edge and alert. It was a long night.

Chapter 18.

As the sun shone through the gaps in the door Ruhsarr sat up. His body ached and his head was sore. He made his way to the river and collected two buckets of water. He returned to the farm and let the animals out in to the field. He emptied a bucket of water into their trough, and they all gathered round to drink. He made his way back towards the house just as the workers were arriving. Theda greeted them as they approached the house. Ruhsarr placed the bucket on the ground for them to fill their cups as they passed.

"Good morning, everyone," he said. "First of all, thank you for coming back. I would have understood if you didn't want to come here today. You all know Dolna disappeared yesterday. Myros told me she had you search the area. Thank you for doing that. Myros, Hark, Theda and I searched for him too when we got back. Sadly we didn't find him either. I want you to work in groups of three from now on. Look after each other and keep in sight of each other. If there are any signs of danger, or anyone else goes missing, raise the alarm and get to safety. I'm going to head into the forest and look for any signs of Dolna. I will be honest with you though I'm not expecting to find him alive," said Ruhsarr. Some of the workers nodded, some looked down at their feet.

"I would like to help you with the search," said Hark.

A few of the other workers stepped forwards and offered their help too.

"Of course. Your help is appreciated," said Ruhsarr.

He and three of the workers walked through the forest carrying tools and weapons for protection. They found blood splashed across the trunks of several trees. They looked around the area and a short distance away they found a piece of skull with an area of scalp and hair still attached. A little further along they found a blood-soaked scrap of a shirt.

"Do you think this was Dolna?" said one of the workers.

They all examined the items. Hark rubbed the back of his hand across his chin.

"This is the same colour as the shirt Dolna was wearing. I think this must be his," he said.

"What are we going to do?" said a worker.

"There is nothing we can do. Sadly Dolna is most probably dead. There is no way he could survive with that much of his head missing. We should go back to the farm and tell the others," said Ruhsarr.

Things were quiet for a few days after Dolna's death. A few of the workers were talking about another farm to the west.

"A bull and two sheep all gone missing and others have been left torn limb from limb," said one of them.

Ruhsarr walked past them across one of the fields and into his house. He took some bread, tore a piece off and stuffed it into his mouth. He was chewing when a scream split the air outside. He dropped the bread and ran out as people were running in panic towards him. The fear was visible on their faces. As he dodged them he saw Myros.

"What is happening?" he said.

He caught her in his arms as she stumbled towards him.

"We saw a…we saw a…"

Theda was running towards him now. She was screaming one word in a drawn out, shrill voice of alert. One word he hoped to never have to hear spoken in fear again.

"Dragon!"

As if on cue a beast flew over their heads carrying a goat in the talons of its hind feet. The animal's head and limbs flailed limp and dead. The dragon let out a long low-pitched roar that shook the air around him.

"Get everyone inside!" He shouted.

He led Myros to the house and sat her down by the fire. Then ran through the house to retrieve the shield Hateish had made him. He slung it over his shoulder and ran back to the door. Theda was ushering the workers into the house. Ruhsarr saw his own fear reflected in their faces, but he had no time to be afraid.

"Keep them calm. When the dragon follows me, lead them back to Aslakvaas," he said to Theda.

"Where are you going?" she said.

"I'm going to draw the thing away," he said.

"Have you lost your mind?" she said

The expression of disbelief was etched across her face.

"Please, just do as I ask," he said.

He didn't wait for her response as he ran out towards the field where the animals grazed.

He ran into the centre of the field but there were no sign of any animals, besides their bull, Hod.

The dragon flew a low circle above the farm. It watched as one of the people ran away from the dwelling place and across the fields. It eyed the thing upon the human's back. It was made of a familiar material. The dragon swooped down for a closer look and realised the human was wearing something made from dragon scales. This was the one the Forest Folk had told him about. The one who refused to leave the land. The dragon flew over the human and threw the goat's carcass at him.

The body crashed into the ground beside Ruhsarr, cascading blood and wet viscera in all directions. He put up his hands to shield his face. As he did the dragon landed heavily just a few feet ahead from him. Ruhsarr moved his hands, and his eyes met those of the dragon. Its large turquoise eyes with silver irises stared deep into his very being. Ruhsarr stepped back and looked the dragon up and down. It drew back the lips of its wide snout to reveal row upon row of long, sharp teeth that ran the length of its upper and lower jaws. The growl it emitted was so deep Ruhsarr felt the sound vibrate through him. Long horns stood out from the sides of its skull and continued until they met at the back of its head. Despite its long neck, it was shorter than the last dragon Ruhsarr had faced, but its huge shoulders were still higher than the top of his head. Its heavily muscled and scale covered front legs led down to hands, each of which bore three fingers. Each finger was tipped with a long black claw. The hind limbs had feet and talons like that of an eagle. Two wings of flesh connecting long finger-like appendages were folding down neatly against its back. The beast's entire body was covered in thick, deep red, scales. It was a formidable beast.

Ruhsarr took a step to the side, and the dragon copied the movement and moved with him. He stepped back and the dragon followed. He quickly realised he couldn't go back to the house. He would be putting everyone in danger if he did. Thoughts ran through his head as he tried to pick a course of action. He stepped to the right but then quickly ran to the left. The dragon tried to follow him but the sudden change in direction caused it to step heavily. The ground beneath its foot gave way, causing it to lose its balance and it crashed down onto its right shoulder. Clumps of dirt and grass were thrown into the air. Ruhsarr ran with all his might as it got to its feet and regained its composure. It chased after the man as he ran. Ruhsarr could hear the roar of the river and see its steep bank. As the dragon closed in on him he fought the urge to stop and leapt from the bank. He plunged into the frigid, fast flowing water. As it swept him along the dragon threw out his wings and flew. His plan was working. Soon the river made its way into the forest. As it curved it passed under a thick area of the canopy. He swam as hard as he could for the inside bank where the water was the slowest and pulled himself out onto the stony ground. He lay there and caught his breath but knew that the dragon would not be far behind. He pulled himself to his feet and ran deep into the thick undergrowth. He heard the dragon fly over. The branches of the trees that criss-crossed over the river exploded. Wood and leaves were thrown in all directions as the huge body of the beast burst down through them. It landed heavily on the banks of the river. It snorted in deep breaths as it swung its head from side to side. Ruhsarr froze, held his breath and listened. The beast was moving away from him, so he moved slowly through the foliage and made his way back towards the farm. An hour later he arrive back on his land. He stepped towards the house and noticed it was silent. Only the animals stirred inside as they heard him approach. As he looked across to the treeline a silhouette above the canopy of the trees caught his eye. It was the dragon. He watched as it circled over the trees. He spoke quietly to himself in a prayer-like way.

"Please don't. Not the hill, not my land," he said.

His heart sunk as he watch the beast descend and then land as graceful as a leaf on top of the hill. He looked down at his feet and whispered.

“Fuck you. I’m gonna fucking kill you too.”

He raised his head, took one more anger filled look at the hill then turned on his heel and continued past his house and on to Aslakvaas.

Chapter 19.

The gatekeeper looked down at Ruhsarr as he approached the gates of Aslakvaas. A meagre smile spread across his face as he looked at the tall blonde bedraggled man. Ruhsarr's hair was thick with mud, his clothes were wet and dirty, and the skin of his face and hands was cut and scratched.

"Where is the dragon?" said the gatekeeper.
Ruhsarr shook his head.

"I don't know. I lost it in the forest. It hasn't followed me if that is what you mean," he said feeling some shame for the lie.

"Theda and your farm hands arrived here some time ago. They are all home safe and well thanks to you. Theda is in the Elder's Hall talking with Tuek. They are waiting for you," he said as he opened the gates.
Ruhsarr stepped through then and nodded his gratitude the man. The nod was returned along with a smile.

Ruhsarr's legs ached as he made his way up the hill towards the high roofed building. He knocked on the door and entered. Theda and Tuek were sat at the far end and sat behind the table. They were talking but Ruhsarr couldn't hear what was being said. As he trudged passed the stone circle Theda looked up at him. She stood up and let the wolf pelt she held around her shoulders fall to the ground. She ran into his arms and planted a firm kiss on his lips.

"We waited until the dragon followed you over the fields to the river. That's when we made our way back here. I'm so glad you are ok. If not a bit of a mess," she said. A smile broke across her face on the last sentence.

Ruhsarr had never seen her look so beautiful. He knew it was probably because he knew how close he had come to not getting back to her, but he didn't mind. He was just happy to be holding her in his arms again.

"When it first landed infront of me in the field I thought I was dragon food. After I jumped into the river it swept me into the forest. The dragon followed me, and I managed to lose it in there. I'm here now with you and that is all that matters. You are right though. I am a mess," he said.

Theda kissed him again and they walked over to Tuek. The old man smiled at them as they approached.

"You must be tired. Please, sit down. Take the weight from your weary limbs. Once again this town is awe of your selflessness. We are grateful for your courage and willing to put other lives before your own," said Tuek.

"I had to keep them safe no matter the cost," said Ruhsarr.

The Elder smiled and placed his hand on Ruhsarr's shoulder.

"That is some I wish more people in this world would do. It is a good attribute to possess. My life would be a lot easier if more people reacted the way you do. Your actions over the years have saved a lot of people," said Tuek.

"I just did what I felt was right for those people and their families. I know if Theda was in trouble and I wasn't there I would hope someone would help her," said Ruhsarr.

Theda looked up at him and squeezed him with the arm she had around his waist.

"What is it with this land that the dragon like so much?" said Tuek.

"I wish I knew," said Ruhsarr.

Another lie. He didn't like how easy he was finding it to lie these days.

"Do you know where it is now?" said Tuek.

"I saw it in the forest. It landed on the same hill the last dragon settled on. It has not followed me as far as I am aware," said Ruhsarr.

"I hope for all our sakes that you are right. What did the dragon look like" said Tuek.

After Ruhsarr had described the dragon in detail Tuek looked at him in the eyes.

"My predecessors kept records to pass on the knowledge of all the known species of animals. From the way you have described the dragon it sounds like a Shen-Garh, a death dragon. They are venomous. When I was a child a man from the town had hunted a deer. A Shen-Garh swooped down to steal his kill. Instead of letting the beast have the animal he tried to chase it away. The beast merely picked him up by the arm and threw him aside. Its teeth shredded the skin of is shoulder. By the time he managed to stumble back here people didn't recognise him. His shoulder, neck, and face were so swollen and bloated with green puss that he looked like a plump caterpillar. He died two days later after his throat had swollen shut. My point is no one has ever been bitten by a Shen-Garh and survived," said Tuek.

Theda looked from one man to the other.

"What are we going to do now," she said.

"We need to put a group of warriors together again, march to the hill and kill it," said Ruhsarr.

Tuek shook his head and looked at Ruhsarr as if he were insane.

"Did you not listen to a word I just said? This is the most dangerous species of all dragons. The last one was a common dragon and not even half the group returned. This is a death dragon, and we don't have enough fighters and warriors to send out against this beast. I have told you before, if the beast has settled on the hill the best thing you can do is abandon the land," said Tuek.

"I will not abandon my land!" said Ruhsarr.

"If the beast has settled there, abandoning it is for the best. The land is as good as lost. There are none among us skilled enough to fight a Shen-Garh: not even you," said Tuek.

"I will not abandon my land. It has been in my family since Aslakvaas was little more than a farm itself. It belongs to me," said Ruhsarr.

"Ruhsarr, see reason! This is a losing battle. Think of your family and your friends. I know you have a strong connection to the land, but you need to let it go. It might be fertile and has taken a lot of work, but it is now sullied. We'll build you a house here in the town. We can find work for you here," said Tuek.

"No! The land is mine. Go back there, confer with the other Elders and send me the warriors I need! It is my land, and I will kill this dragon by myself if I need to!" barked Ruhsarr.

With that he turned and marched out of the Elder's building and into the town centre.

A look of shock sat on Theda's face. She had never heard Ruhsarr speak like that. She had also never heard anyone address one of the Elders in such a manner. She looked at Tuek and a similar look was also on his face. Tears welled in her eyes.

"What are we going to do?" she said.

"I'll talk with the Elders. They will never agree to this though. This is madness. I understand it's all he has left of his parents but if he goes to fight the dragon alone he will not return. Please, go to him. Try to convince him to see that he will not win this fight," said Tuek.

"I will try," said Theda.
They hugged and she followed her husband out of the building.

Ruhsarr strode down the hill into the town. There were people moving back and forth from place to place as they went about their daily business. He stood on the same raised platform he had stood on the day that he and Tuek address the townsfolk six years before.

"People of Aslakvaas, all of you. Hateish the smith, Droober the baker, Yalee the butcher, all of you, gather round," he said.
The people began to approach him while they did he called out for more.

"You know me, I am Ruhsarr Miehyelzah. The dragon slayer. The Farmer. I call you forth again in a moment of crisis. A moment of great need," he said.

"Ruhsarr, stop this. Listen to Tuek!" said Theda as she approached the crowd who were gathering.

"Once again a beast has settled on my land. Once again I implore you to help me," Ruhsarr said.

"Another beast?" said a man.

"Ruhsarr, you can't fight this dragon!" shouted Tuek as he walked down the hill.

"No, not another dragon. Not another dragon!" screamed Droober as he stumbled backwards shaking his head.

"Droober, calm down," said his wife.

"I can't! No! No!" said Droober as he ran off back into his house.

"A dragon? Last time we helped you with a dragon the town lost most of our warriors!" shouted one woman.

"My husband never came back," shouted another.

"Have you not profited from our actions. This town is in danger, and I need your help again!" said Ruhsarr.

"I will not allow you to take the people of this town into a fight they cannot win. It is a death dragon. None who stand against this beast will live!" said Tuek.

"Please, people of the proud and courageous town of Aslakvaas. I appeal to your strong hearts and good nature," said Ruhsarr.

"Abandon the land, Ruhsarr. You will bring only destruction to this town," said Tuek.

"It is my land. It was my father Anzo's before me. The last dragon took him from me. I can't not allow this dragon to take my land," said Ruhsarr as his voice broke into a sob.

"Abandon the land. There is more land you can claim," shouted a man.

"I cannot. I will not!" said Ruhsarr.

"Ruhsarr, please know that we only want the best for you. Abandon the land. Let it go," said Tuek.

The other Elders were walking down the hill towards them, drawn in by the noise of the crowd.

"Please, Elders, help me," begged Ruhsarr.

They all shook their heads.

"Abandon the land," they all said.

Ruhsarr looked out into the crowd and found a friendly face.

"Hateish, please my friend, stand with me. Help me convince them," said Ruhsarr.

The man looked down and shook his head.

"Listen to the people. Abandon the land," he said.

He raised his chin, and his face was held in an expression of pity. He then turned and walked away.

Tears welled in Ruhsarr's eyes. He looked down at Theda. She took his hand in hers and looked down to her feet. He looked into the crowd and saw more faces with expressions of pity, and some even in anger. He looked to Tuek. The old man gave him the same pity filled expression Hateish had. A cold fear washed over him and a pit of sadness formed in his stomach. It was quickly filled by the broiling fires of rage. He looked down at his feet and tears threatened to fill his eyes. He snapped his head up. The rage pulled his features together.

"You cowards. You fucking weak, soulless wretches. I will kill this dragon myself," spittle flew from between his teeth as he spoke. He pulled his hand from Theda's grip and pushed his way through the crowd.

"Ruhsarr, this is madness. See sense before it is too late," said Tuek. His palms were pressed together, his fingers pointed at the man, pleading with him.

But Ruhsarr was already headed towards the gates. Theda made to follow him, but Tuek grabbed her hand.

"Don't go. Stay here where its safe," he said.

"I can't. I'm all he has," she said.

Tuek nodded, "Ok, stay safe," he said and forced himself to release her hand.

She ran out through the gates after her husband.

Chapter 20.

Theda had to run to catch up with Ruhsarr as he strode angrily down the dirt path that led away from Aslakvaas.

"Ruhsarr, wait!" she said.

He continued to walk at the same pace.

"Hey, Ruhsarr. Slow down," she said.

He looked over his shoulder at her with a scowl on his face but continued to walk.

"Hey, you big fucking meat head. Listen to me!" she shouted.

He stopped and turned to her.

The look she saw on his face was not anger but sadness.

"Do you agree with them, that we should leave our land? That we should walk away from everything I have ever known? All that is left of my family?" he said.

She looked him and shook her head.

"Part of me says that we could start again somewhere else. But you know me. I have a defiant streak. And that part of me says that we should fight for what is ours," she said.

Ruhsarr's eyes searched her face.

"So you are on my side?" he said.

"Of course I am. You are my husband. I would take on this whole world with you if I had too. This isn't going to be easy though. We will have to prepare. There can be nothing left to chance," she said.

The sadness lifted from Ruhsarr's face and was replace with a small smile. Theda walked over to him and planted a kiss on his lips.

"Come, we have much to do," she said and took his hand.

They reached the house just before nightfall. Once inside they secured the doors, sat down to eat, and then turned in for the night.

The touch of the warm summer breeze woke Theda from an odd dream. The remnants of which still swam in her mind. Ruhsarr argued with Tuek who was covered in dragon scales. He lunged at Ruhsarr, gouging at his eyes. Blood shot from his torn face with the sound of metal grinding against stone. She sat up and shook her head in an attempt to clear the dream from her mind and found that Ruhsarr was no longer beside her, but the sound continued. Upon getting to her feet she opened the door with the bedding furs still wrapped around her. Ruhsarr was outside sat on a stool. In one hand he held his battle axe. In the other he held a sharpening stone that he rhythmically worked across the blade's edge. She smiled at him. He raised is head to face her. There was an expression of anger and deep concentration on his face. Upon seeing her it gave way to a broad and loving smile.

"Good morning, my lover," she said.

"Good morning, beautiful," he said.

"How long have you been awake?" she said.

"Just before sunrise," he said and continued to sharpen his axe. "Something has changed in the forest. I saw goblin's moving freely among the trees. I counted at least six of them. They must think that the dragon is an omen of some sort," he said.

"Will they head back underground when the dragon is gone?" said Theda.

"I hope so. The last thing we need is the goblins getting brave. There is plenty of land which they could have free reign over. I don't understand why they want this land," he said.

Her lips moved as if she was about to speak but she pressed them shut instead.

They may feel the same about you, thought Theda but then pushed it from her mind.
Ruhsarr stood up and walked to a sheep carcass he had placed on the wood chopping block. He raised the axe up above his head and brought it down through the carcass. The meat and bone were cleaved clean in two.

"I think this one is ready," he said and lifted the two halves of sheep.

"I'd say so," she said as she raised her eyebrows.
He passed her the animal for preparation for the market then wrapped the bear skin over his shoulders. He put his arm through the strap of the large axe and slung it over his shoulder. Slipped his knife into his waist band and slid the handle of his hand axe into his belt. He slung the shield over his other shoulder. He picked up the bag he had prepared earlier containing enough dried meats, fruit and a skin of water to last two days.
They heard approaching footsteps and looked towards the path. A figure approached them dressed in a cloak. The hood covered his head, keeping his face in shadow. There was a large shield slung over his back. Ruhsarr raised his axe into a ready position. As the figure got closer, he raised his hand and pulled the hood away from his head.

"Hateish," said Theda.
She ran and hugged him.
Ruhsarr looked at him with disgust.

"If you have come here to warn me off and tell me to abandon my land, you are too late. You might as well turn around and go home," said Ruhsarr.

"None of those, brother," said Hateish.

"You call me brother after turning your back on me? Brothers don't abandon each other in their time of need," said Ruhsarr.

"Ruhsarr. At least listen to what Hateish has to say," said Theda.

"Ok. Ok," said Ruhsarr.

"Look, I'm sorry about what happened yesterday. My wife is with child. I told her I would stop getting myself into trouble. I'd say almost everyone would consider going off to fight a dragon to be trouble," said Hateish.

Ruhsarr nodded his head in resigned agreement.

"So, why are you here if not to stop me or tell me that you've promised your wife that you are no longer getting into trouble?" he said.

Hateish drew his axe in one hand, his dagger in the other and held his arms out wide.

"Isn't it obvious? I'm fucking coming with you," he said.

"Isn't that getting yourself into trouble." said Ruhsarr.

"It is, but I thought fuck it. We only live this life once, I'm gonna stand with my brother. Also, I'm not dying today," said Hateish.

"You know you won't die today?" said Ruhsarr.

"Yep. That's right," said Hateish.

"How do you know?" said Ruhsarr.

"Because I said so. I tell myself every day that I'm not dying today and, well, I'm still alive aren't I," said Hateish.

A wide smile spread across his face. The corners of Ruhsarr's mouth turned up slowly, reluctantly, and then willingly, he found himself smiling too.

"So, what do you say? Do you forgive me? The sooner you do the sooner we can kick a dragon's arse," said Hateish and held out his hand.

Ruhsarr smiled and took the hand and shook it.

"You are forgiven, my friend," said Ruhsarr.

"Brother," said Hateish.

"My brother," agreed Ruhsarr. "I just need to talk to Theda for a moment."

"Ok. I'll just fill my water bladder from the lake," said Hateish.

Ruhsarr turned and looked Theda in the eye.

"Look, Theda, I know what I am about to do is dangerous, some would say foolish, but it is something I must do. For the honour of my ancestors. However, if I do not return after three days do as Tuek says. Leave this place and abandon the land," he said.

"Do not let defeat enter your thoughts. You are Ruhsarr Miehyelzah. I know you will return to me," she said.

"Always," he said with a smile. "I love you."

"I love you too," she said.

They kissed deep and passionately, then he and Hateish made their way towards the treeline of the forest.

Chapter 21.

As the two friends strode up the hill Ruhsarr furrowed his brow and held his hands clenched tight in fists. A rage that he had earlier hidden from Theda coursed through his body. However he knew he had to save his energy for what lay ahead of them. He tried to keep his thoughts focused but the closer he got to the rocky outcrops of the hill the more the anger seethed within him.

"Cowards! How dare they not help us? All we have done for the town, and they leave us to face this monster alone? We should be on that Elders council. My family has owned this land here for many generations. If I was in charge things would be different. They would be doing my dirty work! You too, the amount of work you have done for them. Selflessly defending the town from all manner of dangers. They owe you, Hateish. They owe you honour and respect," he said.

"I defend the town, and the town looks after me. I know you have your problems with the council and that is understandable. You supply us with food and deserve to be defended by the town. Maybe when we get back we can talk to them about working out a better system. We need a group of people who defend the town and its dependants, including those outside the walls," said Hateish.

"I've never heard you speak so well. Do the council know one their smith and best hunter is also intelligent?" said Ruhsarr.

"They will when I return. I'm trying, you know, to be more the just the muscle," said Hateish.

"So why are you here?" said Ruhsarr.

"I'm good at being the muscle. Also, you and Theda have been good to me over the years, and you need all the help you can get," said Hateish.

Ruhsarr glared at him. Hateish clapped him on the back.

"Save it for the dragon, big man," he said.

Ruhsarr grumbled. They continued to walk.

The mid-morning sun shone bright on the hills, but no birds sang, and no animals stirred. Not even the insects that usually flew around the flowers that bloomed on these hills. But given the current occupier of the cave he was not surprised by this.

Ruhsarr felt the muscles in his legs relax a little as the gradient of the hill began to level out into its plateau. He knew they were close now and a slither of fear tried to wash over him, but he pushed it down and snuffed it out.

"Nervous?" said Hateish.

"I don't get nervous," said Ruhsarr.

"Bullshit. We all get nervous. It's all part of the fun," said Hateish.

Ruhsarr just grumbled in response.

The mouth of the cave was close now. The closer they got the stronger the smell of burnt flesh became. It filled the air, and every breath was heavy with the acrid stench. The two men carefully picked their steps between the bones that surrounded the mouth of the cave. Most of the bones where those of animals both domesticated and wild. They both knew that some of them had belonged to humans.

"What's the plan then?" said Hateish.

"We'll need access it when we get in there but was thinking I'll go for the head and you go for the heart," said Ruhsarr.

"Ok. Sounds solid enough. I never liked plans being too complex anyway," said Hateish.

Ruhsarr reached out his torch and lit it from the burning carcass of a huge bull before proceeding to enter the cave. Memories of this place came flooding back to him. He steadied his mind and pushed on. The deeper they descended the louder the beast's rhythmic breaths became. Huge breaths that reverberated along the walls of the cave around him. He continued a little further and the shape of his mighty foe stood before him.

Its head rested heavily on its huge front legs and its eyes were shut tight. Its tongue hung loose from its mouth and flicked back and forth as it snored. The beast's entire body heaved with every breath. Ruhsarr could feel the sound vibrate through his flesh and bones as he stood in front of the beast. Its deep red scales gave off a subtle glow as they reflected the flames of the torch in the otherwise near dark of the cave. Just like the beast whose scales overlaid Ruhsarr's shield, this was a truly formidable animal.

He quietly slid the axe from his shoulder and took a position to the left of the monster. He nodded to Hateish who already had his axe ready. He stood to the right of the beast, beside its chest. Ruhsarr lined the axe blade up over the dragon's neck, raised the weapon above his head then swung it down with all his strength. Before the axe reached its intended target the beast swung its head to the right. It knocked Hateish off his feet and threw him into the wall. He slid to the ground unconscious. The blade only managed to sever two of the digits on the dragon's left hand. It roared in pain and reared up on its hind legs to its full sixteen feet in height. Ruhsarr side stepped and swung his axe at the exposed belly of the beast. A swift movement from its forelimb knocked Ruhsarr off his feet. He rolled and got up feeling a little dazed. He looked up just in time to see the beast drop on to all four legs and draw in a deep breath. The last dragon had done this, so he knew what was coming. He threw his shield from his shoulder to his hand in one movement, then slammed the bottom edge hard against the ground. A wall of flames struck the scales that adorned the shield and buffeted round him. The heat was incredible and almost unbearable. Eventually the flames relented. Ruhsarr was up again and running at the dragon. He managed to dodge its bleeding left hand and swung his axe at its head. The beast ducked just in time and the axe shattered its horns as it crashed through them. It rushed forwards and head-butted its little aggressor into the air. Ruhsarr's world spun then hit him hard and he found himself on his back with the dragon stood over him. He swung the axe at the beast's head again, but it caught the weapon between its teeth and pulled it from his grip. With a flick of its neck, the axe was sent flying into the cave wall where the head shattered. He quickly drew his hand axe as he got to his feet and swung it at the beast's stomach. The highly sharpened blade spit the dragon's thick scales with ease and a spurt of thick, red blood splattered over him. As he tried to clean the viscous fluid from his eyes everything became dark, and his head was enveloped in something slimy. A heavy crushing sensation ran from each shoulder to his chest as hundreds of blades pierced his flesh. He realised the dragon had his head in its mouth. The pain became even more intense as his feet left the ground. He swung his arms and kicked his legs frantically. He dropped his axe in the struggle, so he swung his fists wildly at the dragon's face. All this movement was sapping his energy. Panic swept over him as he struggled to breathe.

'Is this how I'm going to die?' he thought.

An idea sprang into his mind, and he groped at the beast's face. He found an eye and pushed his fingers against the point where the eyelids met. The beast thrashed it head, and the eyelids tightened.

Eventually his persistence paid off and his hand slid beneath the layers of flesh. He grabbed the eyeball and squeezed with all his strength. The organ ruptured under his grip and the dragon screamed. It shook its head and Ruhsarr was thrown to the ground at the mouth of the cave. He rolled onto his back and drew as much air into his lungs as possible. The dragon roared as blood and thick fluid oozed down its face. With its good eye it looked at the little man lay on the ground. Its lips moved as it made a series of noises that seemed wracked with anger. With that, it jumped high into the air, stretched out it huge wings, flapped them hard and flew away.

Hateish stumbled from the mouth of the cave and slumped down next to Ruhsarr.

"Ah fuck. What happened?" he said.

Ruhsarr could only cough and splutter.

"I better get you back. You need a healer," said Hateish.

He put his shield on the ground and threaded a length rope through the handles. He rolled Ruhsarr onto it and looped the rope over his chest and under his arms.

"This is gonna hurt, but it's better than being left here while I go for help," said Hateish.

Ruhsarr lay on the shield for what felt like hours. The bite marks in his chest began to burn and he clawed at them with his fingers. He writhed and screamed as intense pain surged through every part of his body. Every muscle began to spasm. His jaws clenched so hard that his teeth cracked and broke. The muscles in his is back tightened and spine arched over till his head touched his heels. His arms curled up hard into his chest. This torture continued for half an hour, then as suddenly as it had begun it stopped. Waves of healing warmth flowed over his body. Eventually, he fell into a comfortable unconsciousness. All this time Hateish pulled the heavy, thrashing and contorting weight of his friend. It was the longest and most weary two miles of his life back to the farmhouse. Each and every step was a struggle causing his bones and muscles ached.

Chapter 22.

Ruhsarr woke with a start, as he sat up a yell burst from his mouth. He looked around himself to find that he was lay on his own bedding by the fire and covered with the bear skin.

Theda walked over and knelt next to him with a bowl of stew and a cup of water. Her bright green eyes looked into his and he realised he was safe.

"You're finally awake. You called out just now," she said with a smile.

"How did I get back here?" he asked.

"Hateish dragged you through the door two days ago on your shield after the two of you went to kill the dragon. I feared you might be dead the way you seemed so lifeless. You were covered in blood, and mud, and some sort of slime. When I saw you were still breathing I was so relieved. We cleaned you up and bandaged your wounds, then Skalat he healer from Matchek came and treated your wounds," she said.

"My love, what would I do without you?" he said with a smile.

"You would probably have died years ago," she smirked. "What do you remember?"

Ruhsarr rubbed his head thinking.

"We went to the cave and found the dragon asleep. We fought but, unfortunately, it fled. I dealt it some damage with my axes but obviously he damaged me more," he said.

He touched his hand to his chest expecting to find bandages but found it was bare. The wounds from the dragon's teeth were now almost fully healed. Memories of the aftermath came back to him, and he put his hand up to his face. He felt around inside his mouth with his tongue and found all his teeth to be fine and undamaged. Like the wounds in his chest they had already healed. His mouth turned down in a frown of confusion.

"Is there something wrong?" said Theda.

"It's strange, I remember being wounded. It sunk its teeth into me. It could have bitten my head off, but now I'm healed," he said.

He became agitated but Theda placed her hands on his shoulders.

"Relax, my love. You are safe here. The healer's herbs have done their job," said Theda.

"Yes, Skalat. He does have some good remedies. They seem to be working," he said with a smile as he settled.

"Eat your stew. You'll need your strength," she said and kissed him on the lips. "I have vegetables that need to be picked."

She stood up, walked towards the door, then looked back and smiled at him and left to do her work.

The next day Ruhsarr felt well enough to get up and work. He spent the day making small fixes to the walls of the house. Filling in holes that had been dug in the plaster by animals and insects. By the time he and the farmworkers all sat down to eat he was feeling good. Later the workers returned to their homes in the town. Ruhsarr and Theda put the animals in their pens for the night and settled down by the fire. They roasted a pheasant and ate it, then snuggled together under the animal skins and fell asleep.

They woke with the rising sun and set out into the fields as the workers arrived for the day. Ruhsarr let the animals out into the fields to graze. He herded the horses, cows, goats, and sheep over the fields. Depositing animals by their species and needs in areas along the way. He herded the sheep along to their grazing area and looked up. His house stood in the distance. As the sun beat down on him he stopped for a moments rest. He moved to stand under the shade of a tree when his skin began to tingle all over. He felt odd, like his body was shifting under his skin. Despite the strange sensation he pushed on and continued with his work. The tingle in his skin became a burning sensation and he felt that he was struggling to breathe. He felt lightheaded then fell to his knees. He looked at his hands and saw that the skin was turning white and dry and beginning to flake in moments. His vision became blurry, so he rubbed his eyes, but instead of clearing his vision became opaque. He felt deep, sharp stabbing pains from two points in his back. There came an audible crunch and sudden movements inside his body. There was something solid under his skin. Two lumps pushed up out of his back just below his shoulder blades. The burning sensation shot from his head down to his toes in pulses, like waves of fire. He fell to the ground and lay there. His back and his legs stiffened as the bones began to elongate. It felt like every sinew, ligament and tendon in his body threatened to tear. He tried to cry out, but no sound came. He tried to move but his limbs locked up so tight that that he lay rigid on the ground. The pain became even worse until he couldn't bear the agony any longer and he blacked out.

As he came around he noticed the pain was gone. He hauled himself up to his feet and tried to look around, but he still couldn't see. There seemed to be something in his eyes. He blinked a few times and felt whatever was obscuring his vision become dislodged. A few more blinks and one fell from his left eye. As it floated towards the ground he caught it in his hand. He looked at it for a moment, moving it in his fingers before he realised what it was. What he held in his hand was the layers of skin from the front of his eyeball. He reached up and touched the surface of his other eye with his fingertip. It was rough but delicate, like a wasp's nest. He pinched it between finger and thumb and pulled it away with a light tearing sound. He blinked a few times then looked around. He could see now that the sun had set, and the moon was low on the horizon. In spite of this his vision was better than it had ever been. He looked at his farm and could see every detail with pin sharp accuracy.

"What madness is this?" he said aloud.

His knees buckled and he stumbled back. He dropped the skin to the ground and set off running across the field to his home. As he reached for door his face smashed into the door frame so hard his feet flew up and crashed through the door before he fell to the ground..

'That doorway is higher than me. How did I hit my head?' He thought as he lay there holding his face. Theda jumped up from her place by the fire and backed away from him.

"Who are you?!" she screamed.

"It's me, Ruhsarr," he said.

He stood up but was still holding his face. She picked up one of the sharpened axes and wielded it towards him.

"Do you think I'm stupid? You're taller than my husband. Now tell me who you are, or I'll gut you!" she said.

Ruhsarr lowered his hands to show her his face.

"Theda, please. It is me, Ruhsarr," he said.

She recognised his face and lowered the weapon.

"What? How is this possible?" she said.

But as she approached him the firelight illuminated his eyes, and she recoiled and fell back.

"Did the dragon's bite do this to you? What's happening?" she said.

"What do mean?" he said.

She turned the axe so that he could see the reflection of his face. His skin was white and flaking away, his whole face was dry. But then he saw what had horrified her. His eyes were orange like fire, with no sclera and his pupils were long, vertical slits. His eyes were not human. They were like the eyes of a dragon.

He screamed and he took a step towards her.

"Please, help me," he pleaded in shock.

He stumbled towards her, but she scampered away across the floor. She shook her head, and her face was locked in a grimace of terror. He had never seen her so terrified. He did the only thing that made sense in that moment. He turned and ran from his home into the cold, dark night.

Chapter 23.

Ruhsarr woke to the sun shining on his face and sat bolt upright. As the vestiges of sleep receded from his mind the last echoes of a nightmare faded away. He found that he was lay in a field with the strange taste of iron lingering in his mouth. He became aware of the thing beside him. The carcass of a cow lay on its side in the grass. Its throat had been torn open, and blood caked the now cold flesh surrounding the wound. Ruhsarr looked at his hands and arms and realised he too was covered in the cow's blood. He rubbed his hands in the grass, but it was no use. The blood had dried on and stained his flaking skin.

Somewhere close by a cockerel crowed at the morning sun. Ruhsarr pulled himself to his feet and looked around. There was no one nearby as it was still very early. He was stood close to the shore of a small lake. His mind raced and he was worried someone might see him, so he set off running towards the water. Each stride he took was huge and he was shocked by his own speed. He reached the shore in moments and fell to his knees in the shallow water. He then plunged his hands beneath the surface, lifted handfuls of water and rubbed it over his face. He put his hands into the water again and rubbed them together. What he saw made his head spin as his mind tried to make sense of it. The cracked white skin on his hands started to come away and disintegrate in the water. He lifted them out and held them up infront of his face. The skin on the palms of his hands hung off like the shed skin of a snake. He turned his hands over to look at the backs of them. His nails had turned yellow, and some had fallen off completely. He ran a fingertip over the skin on the back of his left hand. It move with them as if it wasn't attached underneath. He pinched it between his thumb and forefinger and pulled at it. There was no pain as it tore and came away. He fell back in shock at the horror of what he saw. Where the skin had come away he saw his hand was covered in green scales. As he ran his fingers over this new flesh he found it to be hard and rough. He took hold of more skin and it peeled away. Soon his arms were clear of the white skin up to his elbows. For a few minutes he sat in awe of his new scaled flesh.

He remembered the taste in his mouth and wanted it gone. The realisation that something bizarre was happening to him caused him to panic and he plunged his whole head under the surface. He sucked in a mouthful of the liquid, lifted his head and spat it out. It was thick and red with blood. There were also white chunks in this liquid. He plunged his hand into the lake and retrieved some of them. As he raised his hand up and opened it he realised what he held were his teeth. Whimpers of self-pity and blood fell from his mouth. He ran a hand through his hair. It gathered between his fingers and came away in clumps. It brought most of his scalp away with it. He looked at the clumped up mass of hair and flesh in his scaled hand.

"What's happening to me? Am I dying?!" he said.

A bolt of pain surged through his body. Blood poured from his mouth as rows of serrated teeth pushed their way out through the flesh of his gums. Each one was at least an inch in length. Long, black talons pushed out from the tips of his fingers and toes. More horrendous pain shot through his spine like white hot lightning. The two stumps below his shoulder blades shifted and erupted. The skin that covered them split and tore. Blood poured from flesh as it sleuthed away. Two new limbs forced their way out of his body. They resembled long scaled arms with extremely long fingers. When they had reached their full extent the bones locked into place in his back with a click. The fingers splayed out to reveal they were connected by a thick membrane of skin. He was powerless to stop this transformation all the while he could hear himself screaming in terror.

"I beg the gods, what have I done to deserve this agony?!" he cried.

He knelt there in the water for what to him felt like hours as his body reshaped itself. Finally, the pain began to recede, and his laboured breaths rasped through his new clenched teeth.

He craned his neck to look over his right shoulder and then the left trying to look at these strange new limbs. He watched them move around him so that the fingers were held out infront of him in the way a pair of arms would if he were looking from one palm to the other. It dawned on him that these limbs were responding to his thoughts just as his other limbs did. He moved them slowly at first then stretched them out wide and up over his head. He then folded them down. They sat neat and close against his back. He hung his head and began to quiver slightly, when he raised his head again there was a smile on his face.

"I have wings," he said to himself.

He stretched the wings out and looked at them and then up to the sky. All the anguish and pain he had felt up to now was replaced with wonder and excitement. He moved the wings so that they were pointed straight out from his back. He then brought them forward with force and was thrown backwards off his feet over the pebbled shore. His feet dug into the loose surface, and he was flipped head over heels then landed on his face.

He picked himself up and swept himself off. As he did he noticed something hung round his neck. He pulled it out infront of him and in a moment of horror he realised what he held. It was the skin from his face. He pulled and it came away in his hands. It dangled there like a mask made of shed snakeskin. His hands trembled as a light breeze caught the skin. It bellowed out and took the shape of his face before he let it slip from his grip. In a panic he ran back to the water and looked down at his reflection. The image that looked back at him was a bald headed man covered in scaled skin with no ears and no nose, just nostril slits. He reached a scaled hand to his face and felt his fingertips slide over his cheek. This new skin had the texture and made a sound similar too pebbles sliding over each other. He stood up and tore wildly at all of his clothes until he was naked. He scrapped and tore at his limbs and torso until all the dried skin was gone. He looked down at himself. He was no longer a man. He stood seven feet tall with a pair of wings and was covered from head to toe in dark green scales. He was a humanoid with the qualities of a dragon. He fell to his knees and looked into the water.

"My face! What has become of me? Theda will never even want to look at me again."

He sat on the shore and cried. His mind raced at an unbelievable speed and seemed mere inches from insanity. The transformation was occurring in his mind as well as his body. A strange calm fell over him. As his mind altered he began to accept his grotesque transformation. Thoughts of Theda ran through his mind as tears ran down his face. A thought echoed around in his mind.

"This wouldn't have happened to me if Theda had

taken me in. She turned her back on me. But she was holding me back. I am better now. I am magnificent," it said.

He found a strange comfort in this thought. With this new mind set his thoughts turned back to the possibility of flight. He thought about when he had seen the dragon take off and the way it moved. He got to his feet then crouched down. In this position he concentrated all his strength into his legs and pushed off the ground with all his might. The jump propelled him straight up and high above everything around him. He threw out his wings then swung them down hard and raised them back up. He repeated this flapping motion and soon it felt natural.

'This is what a young bird taking its first flight must feel like,' he thought.

He clumsily started to move forward. Soon he was moving at a good pace. He lowered the left wing and at the same time raised the right and arced off to the left. He lowered the right and raised the left and arced to the right. This new ability took him some time to get used to but soon it was almost instinctive.

Chapter 24.

He had flown across the skies for what seemed around an hour but was actually more like three. He saw his home as no one before him ever had. Huge expanses of forest covered the land and climbed the feet of mountains. The long rivers cascaded down mountains and wound their way through deep valleys. Here and there stood villages, walled towns and farmlands. He never knew the world would look this beautiful from this height. This was the territory reserved for insects, birds, and most of all dragons. Now he had the privilege of this space too. He looked down and saw the village of Aslakvaas which lay just beyond his farmland. He saw the line of the fifteen foot wooden wall in its entirety. He saw the hill and the hall of the Elders at the top.

The sun had risen to its highest point now and the village was alive with people from the surrounding areas. He could hear the chatter of their voices and the fall of their feet. He flew down to get a closer look. He could hear the blacksmiths hammering metals to make tools and blades, the merchants calling to customers, singing voices, and instruments playing. There were people dancing while other people were working and tolling. He could smell the meats on the butcher's stall, the fish on the fishmongers, and the baking of bread. All the things that make a town centre brim with life. A scent wafted up to him. The smell of the people, a scent of life. There was something within that smell, something else that pulled him in, something that beckoned to him, that made his mouth water, and his hunger flair.

He manoeuvred to circle over the town and came down to land. This was the first time he had tried this, and he realised too late that he didn't know how. The full weight of him hit the ground hard and he crashed through a stall of vases. Broken pottery and splinters of wood were thrown in all directions. He got to his feet and momentarily forgot that he no longer looked like the people around him. A woman screamed and the crowd of people looked towards her. They looked past her and saw the seven foot tall monster stood in the splintered ruins of a broken stall. He looked up and saw the crowd turn their backs to him as they fled. The instinctive predatory urge to chase took over and he found himself running after these people. He swung out an arm and grabbed a man by the shoulder, then with little effort he lifted him off the ground. The man fought and screamed as Ruhsarr's claws sank into his flesh. Blood began to flow from the wounds and the scent of it hit Ruhsarr's nostrils. He now understood this was what had drawn him here in the first place. It had made him forget himself and what he had become. The scent that had roused his hunger was that of human blood. He could see it through the man's skin as it pumped through his arteries and veins. He lifted the man to his face and was overwhelmed with an urge to bite him. He gave into it and bit deep into the man's neck. Blood gushed into his mouth. For a moment he was taken aback by the force of it, and it spilled down his chest. Then he gulped it down like nectar. Soon the man's blood pressure dropped. Ruhsarr had to suck the remaining blood out of his victim. He dropped the lifeless body to the ground like discarded rubbish. Unbeknown to him, as he walked away the body began to twitch. Hunger pangs surged through him. He no longer saw people around him, he saw prey. He chased the crowd and grabbed a woman, tore into her flesh and drained her of blood just like he had done to the man. After her the thirst took control and he grabbed and drained person after person until his thirst was quenched.

In all there were eight bodies devoid of blood lay around him on the ground. They began to writhe like they were racked with pain. The first male he had attacked stood up, threw his head back and screamed. Blood poured from the corners of his mouth as fangs burst from his gums. His flesh bulged and shifted as the internal structures of his body began to change. His physique became lean and muscular, and his skin became smooth. Soon the others were getting to their feet too. They writhed and screamed as their bodies went through their own transformations. They were all changed now and stood in front of Ruhsarr, no longer as humans, but as something else. Their skin was pale and had a luminescence to it. It was also partially translucent in the late morning sun. It was not only their bodies that changed, their minds were altered too. They all looked upon Ruhsarr with a look of adoration in their eyes then lowered their heads.

"Master," they said in unison without moving their mouths.

He looked upon these people and it dawned on him that they were bound to him. He could feel some sort of ethereal tether that attached them to him. That he could guide them, converse with them wordlessly across their minds. They would obey him and answer his commands. As the dragon's bite had changed him, his bite had enforced an alteration upon them too. While not as dramatic as his own, in his eyes they had transformed them into something better. They looked stronger and healthier. Their muscular physique and posture was improved. They raised their heads and looked up at him. He saw awe and admiration in their eyes. They looked at him the same way he had seen people look at the Elders.

They looked at him as though he was a god.

"What will you have us do, Master?" said the first female aloud.

The blood was altering the physiology of Ruhsarr's brain. Twisting his mind and breaking down his sense of morality. He felt intoxicated by it, and he could feel the power he had over these people. His scaled lips pulled back from his sharp, blood soaked teeth in a vicious smile. Twisted and barbaric thoughts ran through his ravaged mind.

"Kill them all," he said.

His voice was deep, bold, and guttural, like a bear who had learned to speak with human words.

"Yes master," they said.

They reared up into attack stances and chased the villagers. Most of who had already found or were in the act of trying to find somewhere to hide. His followers dragged people from under mounds of hay, and out from wells. They kicked down doors and dragged screaming families from their homes. Ruhsarr revelled in the pitiful screams of the humans as their bodies were wrenched apart, their blood was drunk, and their lives were torn away from them. Their cries for mercy were ignored as they were snuffed out like candles.

As he walked in the direction of these screams he saw one of his followers run up the hill to the Elder's Hall. Ruhsarr ran to him and placed his hand on the male's shoulder.

"These are mine to kill," he said.

"Yes, my master," said the male,

He smiled up at Ruhsarr and ran back down the hill. He leapt on to the back of a man who had stabbed one of the females with a pitchfork. He wrapped his hand around the man's head with his fingers under his jaw and pulled. With a bloody crunch and the sound of tearing flesh the head was liberated from the man's body.

Ruhsarr strode towards the doors of the Elder's Hall. He kicked them open so hard they splintered and broke from their hinges. As he stepped inside the wind swirled dust in around him. The air inside was thick with the scents of burning herbs and sacrificial animals. He could sense the blood as it moved through their veins. As he walked through the circle of stones he dragged his claws across the surfaces of the ones closest to him carving gouges into their rough surface.

The four guards ran out and placed themselves between him and the five Elders sitting at the back of the building. One approached pointing a spear at him and opened his mouth to speak. Before he could Ruhsarr snatched the spear, flipped it over and pushed it through his chest. He lifted the dying guard from the ground, took two quick strides towards another guard and thrust the spear through his head. He dropped the two skewered guards to the ground. The next two guards stepped towards him swinging their axes. One of which he dodged while he threw a punch that connected with the guard's face and pulverised his skull. The last guard was the only one of the four to actually hit him with a weapon. The axe cut into the scales of his shoulder but drew no blood. With the hand of the same arm Ruhsarr snatched the man by the throat and lifted him off the ground. With a flick of his wrist he inverted the man and slammed his head into the hard ground shattering his head and spine.

The Elders all gasped at the speed and brutality of the attack. Heg, Golm, and Vito stood up from their chairs and were about to head into the room behind them.

"You know as well as I that there is nowhere to go in that room. The only way out now is to pass me.

So, sit down!" said Ruhsarr.

His voice boomed on the last two words, and the Elders felt an overwhelming compulsion to obey his words. Some of them whimpered as they retook their seats.

Turk spoke and tried to keep his voice steady.

"I am Tuek, oldest of the five Elders of Aslakvaas! How dare you enter this sanctum, this sanctuary! Only a demon would kill in a chamber of peace?!"

"Demon?" said Ruhsarr as a smile played across his lips. "Oh no, I am no demon."

"What are you then, if not a demon?" said Tuek.

Ruhsarr continued his approach.

"I thought you would at least recognise me. It was you after all who condemned me to this. When you refused to help me to fight that dragon you sealed my fate," said Ruhsarr.

He was close enough now for them to see him better as the fires cast their light across his face. Elder Drassi gasped and put her hand to her mouth.

"Does my appearance disgust you? Do you fear me, or have you just realised the consequences of your betrayal?" he said as he strode ever closer.

"Ruhsarr?" said Tuek.

"You do recognise me," said Ruhsarr with a grin.

"What has become of you? What horrors have the gods inflicted upon you?" said Tuek

"You would not give me help when I needed it. Now, the dragon has made a monster of me. This is not the work of the gods. It is all your doing!" said Ruhsarr.

"You cannot put the blame of this tragedy on us!" said Heg, to the left of Tuek.

The smile on Ruhsarr's lips fell away and was replaced with a deep scowl.

"Oh, but I do blame you. I blame all five of you little cowards!" said Ruhsarr.

His voice boomed and echoed around the building.
He moved across the remaining space in one swift movement and grabbed Heg by the head. The man reached up too late. Ruhsarr squeezed his hand tightly until it popped like a melon. Then shook the skull and brain fragments from his open hand. Around Tuek the three remaining elders stood up from their seats. Ruhsarr jumped on Drassi, grabbed her head and with ease he tore it off her neck with an audible crack. He threw it at Vito as he ran away. It hit him square in the back and sent him sprawling to the stone floor. Ruhsarr flew through the air and landed on the man's back. He gripped Vito by the shoulders and pulled upwards until the man's back broke in three places. Splinters of bone shot out through his flesh. Golm, the last female Elder, sprinted at full pace towards the doors. Just as she reached them something crashed into her back, and she was lifted off the floor. She looked down and saw a huge bloody, scaled hand protruding out through her chest. Its fingers were wrapped around her heart. Ruhsarr heard Tuek call his name from the back of the building. He cast Golm's lifeless body to the floor and turned around to face Tuek who was still seated. Ruhsarr strode quickly back towards the feeble, old man and licked the blood from his hand as he did.

"Why are you doing this to us!?" said Tuek.

"Why?!" Roared Ruhsarr. "Look at me you fool!"

"I didn't realise we had sent you to such a horrific fate, Ruhsarr. Please. Don't let any more blood spill today," said Tuek.

"Your betrayal should have cost me my life, but instead, I was transformed. It was excruciating. I should have been destroyed, but I was remade. I am starting to like what I have become," he said.

He grabbed Tuek and threw him across the open

floor of the building. The old man landed near the circle of stones. Ruhsarr strode over, wrapped his arms around one of the stones that stood eight feet tall. He pulled it up out of the ground and held it above his head.

"See. I am stronger than I have ever been!"

"Ruhsarr, I-I implore you. G-Go and kill the dragon. Maybe its death will reverse this curse," said Tuek.

"Listen to me, Tuek. If you had done so in the first place I would not be the beast you see before you and none of this death and bloodshed would have been necessary. Even if slaying the dragon does work, you will not see it. Do you know what I am, Tuek?"

Tuek meekly shook his head.

"I am the Trahhogod, the Dragon Lord, the god of death, and today I rain my wrath down upon you," said Ruhsarr.

"No, please! No!" said Tuek in a voice that broke into a scream.

Ruhsarr dropped the stone onto the old man. Its weight flattened him completely beneath it.

Ruhsarr turned and walked to the door of the elder's hall. As his newfound abilities continued to improve he felt alive and unstoppable, he felt reborn. He stepped out into the fresh air and an axe buried itself into his stomach. The man wielding it tried to wrench it free, but he grabbed the head of it and held it in place. He looked down and saw the face of his attacker, a face he recognised.

"Hateish?" he whispered.

Another axe swept towards his jaw. He managed to throw his head back just in time and the blade only grazed his chin. Hateish released the axe that was buried in his stomach and reached for a long dagger in his belt. As Ruhsarr lowered his head Hateish reached up and plunged the dagger into his face just below his left eye. Despite his newfound abilities he could still feel pain, and this was agony. He thrashed his head around and swung his clawed hand in Hateish's direction. The man was nimble for his size, and he took a quick step back. Ruhsarr took hold of the dagger handle and pulled it free. The wound closed up immediately.

"The people of this town helped you and this is how you repay them!?" snarled Hateish.

Ruhsarr stepped closer and thrust the blade towards Hateish's throat, but it was knocked from his hand by an axe. As he watched the dagger fly Hateish ducked under his arm and pulled the other axe free from his stomach. He bellowed in pain and swung a balled up fist at Hateish, but again he ducked. The man stepped around Ruhsarr, straightened up and swung both axes towards his lower back. Ruhsarr flicked out a wing that caught Hateish in the chest and knocked him off his feet. He hit the floor hard feet away.

"They betrayed me! I am repaying them in kind," said Ruhsarr.

Hateish glared at him from the ground.

"I'm going to put your head on a spike," said Hateish.

"Come and try, old friend," growled Ruhsarr, and beckon to him mockingly.

Hateish was up on his feet and lunged wildly within a moment. Ruhsarr tried to step back but Hateish's axe was already slicing the air towards his head. Ruhsarr turned away from the weapon as it bit into the back of his neck. Blood arced out from the wound, He howled and thrashed around, lashed out and threw Hateish aside. The man landed on his side and rolled. He looked at Hatish and strode towards him. He reached down to grab him, but Hateish quickly rose up to one knee and swung out an axe that took off Ruhsarr's reaching fingers. As he reeled back looking at the stumps Hateish rose to both feet and swung the other axe towards Ruhsarr's left knee. He moved his leg, but the axe caught his shin and knocked him off balance. He spun with the momentum and used it to backhand Hateish across the head, sending the man stumbling forwards. Ruhsarr raised his hand and saw the bones and tendons that held them together regrowing from the stumps of his fingers. Muscle fibres were growing over them in layers along with skin and scales. He looked down and saw the skin of his stomach had knitted itself back together. He turned and looked at Hateish, who shook his head as he watched in terror.

"It looks like the spike will be for you," said Ruhsarr.

Hateish stepped forwards and swung an axe, but Ruhsarr caught the handle and wrenched it from his hand. He snapped the head from the handle and cast the parts aside.

"Fuck!" roared Hateish.

He swung his remaining axe, but Ruhsarr knocked it from his hand. The two of them looked at each other for a moment and then Hateish took a quick step towards the weapon that now lay on the hard packed ground. Before he could reach it Ruhsarr shot out and hand and grabbed him by the throat. He held Hateish in front of him and for a moment their eyes met and he remembered something. This man who struggled and tried to break free of his grip was his friend.

"Hateish. We stood together, fought together. We don't need to do this," he said.

"You always were a cunt," said Hateish.

A sad smile curled just the very corners of Ruhsarr's mouth. He knew that Hateish wouldn't stop until death. He squeezed his hand shut. Hateish's eyes rolled back in his head as the life was crushed from him. Ruhsarr gently lay the body of his friend, his enemy down, on the ground.

"I wish this could have been different he said. Then he stood and called out to his followers. They stopped attacking the town's people and gathered round him. He noticed that there were more of them now. Maybe ten to twelve. In all the excitement he had not thought about counting them. The devotion was visible in their eyes.

"Follow me. We have a new hunt to pursue" said Ruhsarr.

"Where do you lead us to, Master?" said one of the females.

"To the forest. We're going to kill a dragon," he said.

They walked down the hill into the decimated town. Broken bodies and dismembered limbs lay all around, blood was splattered over everything, and houses burned.

Not too far from them but hidden behind the wall of a partially collapsed building stood Theda. She held her axe in her hands and there were tears in her eyes.

"Oh, my love, what has become of you?" she said quietly to herself.

Even though her voice was barely a whisper Ruhsarr heard her, and he turned to listen. He strained his ears in an attempt to hear her again.

"What is wrong master?" said one of his followers.

"Be silent and stay here," he said.

He walked slowly towards the building behind which Theda stood. She held her breath as she heard him approach. His head was held forwards and his shoulders were held back as he waited to hear any noise that would give her away. Theda nervously adjusted her grip on the axe and readied herself. She flexed the arm with which she held the axe at the elbow and rotated her wrist. She could hear his breath as it rasped between his cruel teeth. Then she raised the head of the axe over her shoulder and steadied her hand on the handle. She sprang out from her hiding place and lunged at Ruhsarr.

"Theda?" he said.

Tears rolled down her face as she swung the weapon at his chest. It sliced through his scaled flesh, and she was showered with his thick blood. He roared in pain, but the wound started to heal instantly. Closing shut as if it was being fastened with a zipper. She swung again but he caught the axe. He tried to pull it from her hands, but she held on, so he lifted her from the ground. In a movement which took her by surprise he took hold of her around the waist with one hand and pulled her free from the weapon.

"Unhand me you vile fiend, you monstrous abomination!" she said.

Ruhsarr's lips curled up to bare his teeth. He placed his clawed finger under her chin.

"Why are you so angry at me? I am your husband," he said.

"You are not my husband," she said in a whisper.

Ruhsarr grimaced and pushed his finger up against the skin of the underside of her jaw. The claw sliced through the flesh and his finger pushed her tongue aside as it entered her mouth. She let out a garbled cry of agony as blood filled what space was left in her mouth. With a flick of his wrist her jaw tore away at the left joint. Blood poured from her ripped open face as a wail escaped her throat. She went limp in his hands as she passed out. In an act of callous abandonment he dropped her motionless body to the ground and spat on her cheek.

"And you are no longer my wife," he said mockingly.
With that he called to his followers, and they walked away from the town leaving a trail of bodies and destruction in their wake.

Chapter 25.

It was midafternoon by the time Ruhsarr and his followers reached the hillside where he fought the first dragon and had his fateful encounter with this current dragon. This place was engrained in his mind. He had been able to see this hill from his land since he was a small child. It was a place he had walked to on many occasions. He had come here with Anzo to hunt many times throughout his life. He could have found this place blindfolded. But now the fondness he had felt for this place was gone. The death of his parents and the loss of his humanity had etched scars through all the memories he held of this land. Even now though, he wasn't prepared to give it up. This was a fight he was going to see all the way through until the bitter end. He looked around surveying the area. He snorted the air deep into his lungs. Even through the stench of the burnt and half eaten carcasses at the mouth of the cave he could smell the sulphurous scent of the dragon. A sound rang from deep inside the cave. It started as the loud, deep growls of the dragon but the sounds started to form words that made sense to Ruhsarr's altered mind. The beast spoke in the old language of the ancestors but in a long, low, drawn out frequency that vibrated the air all around him.

"Ah, I see the self-proclaimed enemy has returned as my strange beastly offspring," It spoke with the air of intelligence and grandeur. "So, you come to trouble me once again with your presence."

"I come to slay you, vile beast!" Ruhsarr said with a snarl.

The Dragon made its way out from the mouth of the cave. Its red scales gleamed like jewels in the sun.

"Vile beast? Me? Have you seen your reflection of late? I may be a beast to humans but vile I am not.

I'll have you know I am one of the most handsome dragons who has ever lived. You on the other hand, you are a detestable abomination. Neither human nor dragon. Tell me, what do you think you are, besides a monster?" said the dragon with a grin.

"Rest your flapping jaw. You are a fiend, and I have come to rid this land of your wretched existence," said Ruhsarr.

"Oh, so that is why you bother me in my home once again. Last time you did this you were little more than a minor irritation. By the looks of things, you may be a little more than human. Aside from that, it is you and your little minions whose existence in this land is wretched. I know you think you are some kind of force to be reckoned with now, but really, you are not much of anything. I know what you did to the innocent people of that village. You are a hornet throwing its weight around in a beehive. A monster, but only to those smaller than you," said the dragon.

"Are you going to pretend you are something aside from one of the animals of this land? Like you haven't eaten herds of livestock, or humans too? What about all the carcasses out here?" Ruhsarr said in an attempt to sound clever.

The dragon blew a snort of annoyance from its nostrils and stood up to its full height.

"I ate the livestock because I was hungry. I ate two humans because they tried to attack me whilst I slept. Your similar actions led to your current predicament. Although I must say, I certainly never expected you to survive. The carcasses are here to deter humans. Though evidently, they don't work on the foolhardy and the idiotic. I did not kill them for sport, I killed them out of necessity, because I must eat. I most certainly didn't kill them as part of an inept, ill thought out, rage filled act of revenge!"

The dragon craned its head down to look Ruhsarr right in the eye.

"I'm gonna tear out your heart!" Snarled Ruhsarr.

"I am Azangor, I have existed on this earth and flown its skies for thirty thousand years. Many have tried to defeat me. None have succeeded. That will not be changed by an infectious, half breed, freak of nature, and his infected imps!"

Ruhsarr let out a roar and ran at the dragon. It grabbed him by the head and slammed him down hard into the ground. He got right back up and threw himself at the beast. This time Azangor delivered a punch to his chest that sent him flying back across the stony ground. Again, Ruhsarr jumped to his feet.

"Attack him!" he called to his followers.

Two of his followers charged at the dragon. Azangor drew his head back, then lunged forward. A huge ball of fire burst forth from the dragon's mouth. Their flesh ignited immediately as the fire struck them. Ruhsarr was caught in the flames and threw his hands up in self-defence. He screamed as they enveloped him, but he felt nothing, not even the heat. The flames seemed to buffet round him and he realised his scales were fireproof just like the dragon's. He lowered his hands and saw that, unfortunately, his followers were not. They twisted, writhed and screamed as they were engulfed in huge columns of flame. They burst into chunks of charred flesh that shattered to ash as they hit the ground. Ruhsarr looked at the dragon and smiled.

"You'll have to try harder than that, beast."

"Worry not, fiend, I can do this all day," said Azangor.

With that he ran at Ruhsarr and grabbed him by the head. Swung him up and caught his ankles in the other hand. With him held above its head the dragon pulled hard in opposite directions. Its strength was enormous. Ruhsarr screamed as unspeakable pain fired through every nerve of his body. He could feel every sinew, tendon, and muscle tear away from the bones. His mind threatened to leave his body in an attempt to escape, but suddenly through the pain he was aware of a strange clarity. He grabbed the dragon's hand and dug his claws deep into its flesh. Hot blood gushed from the wounds. The dragon roared and let go of his head but still swung him by his feet. It smashed him into the ground with unspeakable force. Smashing his head against a huge rock buried in the hillside over and over again until it broke from his body and hung on by threads of flesh. His back was a mangled wreck of torn flesh and broken bones. Azangor drop his limp body to the ground and turned to Ruhsarr's followers.

"See! Your master is dead! Now leave me in peace, or I will burn you all alive!" he said.

Ruhsarr's body lay broken and surely dead. His followers stood, tears rolling down their faces. Some of them staggered around while others fell to their knees. Their master was dead, and their new lives were already in ruins. It was all over. From where they were stood they didn't see the blood that poured from his wounds beginning to clot. They did, however, see his limbs begin to twitch and move. His tendons and muscle fibres waved like worms as they reached for the bones. Whereupon finding them, they reattached, and his flesh fused back together. He struggled and writhed as the bones of his spine realigned themselves. Popping and crunching as they shifted back into their proper place. He pulled himself to his feet and stood up, but his head still hung down his back, swinging back and forth with his every movement. His followers cheered and danced. The dragon saw them celebrate, looked at him and growled. Ruhsarr's head jerked back into place as the vertebrae of his neck were pulled back together by muscle and tendon. The flesh of his neck fused back together as if it had never been broken. His eyes opened, he drew in a deep breath and let out a deep, rumbling roar. The dragon lunged at him, but he threw a well place punch that connected perfectly with the dragon's jaw. Its head swung to the side and teeth flew from its mouth. He grabbed the dragon's neck, jumped up, and then slammed its head down into the same rock it had smashed him against. The dragon lay dazed on the ground. He lifted up its head and smashed it back down on to the rocks with a crunch. The dragon raised his hand, grabbed Ruhsarr and threw him off, then rolled and stumbled back to his feet. The moment he was stable Ruhsarr punched him in the head. The dragon spun and turned around to see Ruhsarr about to land another punch. He caught him by the head and threw him straight up into the air so high that the land below him fell away. The sensation of spinning into the sky shocked Ruhsarr but he soon stopped ascending and began to fall. He flicked his wings out and was just starting to fly when something silent hit him and tore his wings apart. He saw a flash of the dragon's tail as he fell again. His wings began to heal. The flesh between the fingers was reforming when he was hit hard from above. The impact shattered has pelvis and legs. He let out a cry of pain. The dragon grabbed him, spun in the air and threw him. He was dazed and confused, then he was hit again. He felt the dragon's hands grab him and they fell together. Ruhsarr punched at the dragon's neck until it let him go, opened its wings and backed off. He realised it wasn't the dragon moving away, but he who was still falling. He looked down and slammed into the ground face first. He lay broken and coughing up blood in an impact crater of his image. The dragon came down and landed next to him with a loud thud.

"Do you give up little dragon man?" It said. Ruhsarr let out a moan. He pushed himself up, feeling the bones of his arms knit back together as he did. His wounds were healing fast, but he had lost a lot of blood. The dragon knelt over him and looked him in the eyes.

"Tear my heart out will you? You've been little more than an irritation," Azangor said and grinned It quickly leaned down towards him with the intention of biting off his head, but Ruhsarr grabbed its jaws. With all his strength he forced its mouth open wide until its lower jaw broke with a snap. He then twisted it, feeling the bones grind and break even more. The dragon roared in pain. He pulled back his arm and punched the roof of its mouth. The force knocked Azangor off its feet. It landed on its back and the ground shook. He jumped onto its chest and slashed at the scales with his claws. The dragon swiped at him, but he dodged and dug his claws deep into the muscles of its chest. He threw out his wings and with a lot of effort and flapping he lifted the dragon upwards. He looked down and saw that the trees below seemed tiny. He could see Aslakvaas in the distance to his left. He stopped flapping his wings and they fell together. Before they hit the ground he moved, wrapped his arms around the dragon's neck and put his feet on the underside of the dragon's head. They hit the ground with a sickening crunch. The dragon's skull took all the impact and Ruhsarr's feet went deep into its brain. Its shattered head lay in the broken ground. Its body was mostly still with only slight muscle twitches in its limbs. He got back on its chest, sunk his fingers into the flesh and tore through the layers of muscle. He found he had to work fast as the dragon's healing abilities were greater than his. Its head was already reforming. He slammed his fists into the ribcage until it broke. He pulled away the broken chunks of bone, then pushed his hand in and took hold of the large beating heart and pulled. The dragon grabbed his hand tight and spoke in its low voice with more conviction than Ruhsarr had ever heard from anyone or anything.

"Know this, Ruhsarr. You are nothing more than an accident, a mistake, a scar upon this Earth. You may kill me now, but not before I place a curse upon you and every abomination that you make. They may be stronger since you infected them with your disease, but I bind them with an affliction to the power of the sun. Its light and the pure elements of the earth will wreak havoc upon their corporeal forms. As punishment for your bloodlust, that will be their only sustenance. As for you, your bite will infect a woman who is with child and bearing twins. Her offspring will be transformed. One will be kin to your abominations, the other will be something far more dangerous. I, Azangor, gift this infant to the earth. They will be the embodiment of my curse upon you. They will rise! All whom you infect will perish by their hand. They will scour you from this Earth. They will be your destroyer!"

Ruhsarr had heard of the devastating power of a dragon's curse when he was a child. His grandfather would tell tales around the fire of entire towns wiped from the land due to those afflicted by a such a curse. At this moment he was lost in his arrogance and rage. He saw the dragon's flesh was closing around his wrist. The heart beat a powerful rhythm in his hand. He knew had to finish what he had started. He tightened his grip and pulled with all his strength until it tore free from its holdings within the dragon's chest. He thrust it into the air, held it above his head and roared, long and loud. His followers danced for his recovery and cheered for his victory. He brought the heart down, looked at it, then took a bite out of it and swallowed it whole. This was the last thing the dragon saw, its head then fell back, and its body became limp. Ruhsarr swallowed down the rest of the heart in chunks. His stomach lurched as what felt like a bolt of lightning shot through his body. He threw his head back and roared again but this time the pitch was much deeper. All his limbs began to shake. The bones within his flesh rumbled and extended, while his muscles strained and stretched under his scaled skin. He felt the sensation that he was getting taller and bigger. He now stood seven feet seven inches. All his senses improved to an even higher level than they already were. He became aware of the way the increased number of filaments of dazzling sunlight lit the leaves of different trees in different ways. As he breathed in his nose caught the scents of the forest carried upon the wind, and along with that he smelt the scent of decomposition. He realised it was coming from the dragon's body. The initial stages of decay had already begun. He watched as its blood seeped into the earth and knew he had to act fast. He looked around and found a large, kiln fired vase. The type that were used to store mead. He picked it up and carried it to the dragon's body. Then, using all his strength, he heaved the bulky carcass onto is shoulder. He held it there, over the vase while the blood poured into it from the wound in the chest. When it was full he unceremoniously dropped the dragon's body and used his claws to cut a sheet of skin from one of the wings. He placed this over the mouth of the vase. He tore a tendon from the same wing and tied it around the top to hold it in place and seal the vessel.

His followers quickly approached him.

"The curse, Master. It has begun already. Help us," said one of the women.

"The sun. We're burning," said the other.

He turned and saw the skin of his remaining followers had started to blister in the sun.

"This way," he said.

He quickly ushered them all into the cave.

"Please Master. I am scared," said one of the women.

"You have no need to fear. The gift I have given you has made you strong. What is your name?" he said.

"Gilad," said the woman with a smile.

"Gilad, I will lift this curse and give you all many more gifts. We will rule over the humans together," he said with a smile.

His followers all looked up to him with pure admiration.

"Your master is good to you, yes?" he said.

"Yes Master, you are kind and wise," they all said.

He smiled at them and his ego grew as his mind twisted in grotesque and horrifying ways.

Chapter 26.

The next morning the sun rose over the village of Aslakvaas. The bodies of the townspeople remained where they had fallen. Flies buzzed round them as the first signs of decomposition set in.

In a house on the edge of the town three people huddled together in silence. Sunlight filtered through the gaps in the pile of wood they had used to barricade the door. It was a relief to see daylight after the long cold night.

"The sun has risen. I can't stand too just sit here and wait anymore. I'm going to find help," said Attoot.

He stood up, stretched his muscles and shook his head of long black hair.

"Please don't, it's too dangerous. They might still be out there," said Marriat.

"My love, I have to I need to warn the surrounding villages. You stay here and look after Valetice. All being well, I'll be back tomorrow," said Attoot.

He removed some of the wood from the barricade and slipped out of the door. Marriat hung onto his arm. They both flinched as the early morning air was thick with the smell of decay.

"Stay inside and block the door after I have gone. Stay low and stay quiet. I love you," said Attoot.

"I love you too," she said and kissed him.

She closed the door and with the help of Valetice they piled the wood back against the door. They then sunk to the floor and huddled together.

Outside Attoot took a few cautious steps away from the house. The only sound was the buzzing of flies. His confidence grew when he saw an axe on the ground and walked towards it. Something moved behind him, and he froze. He slowly looked over his shoulder and what he saw made his heart pound against his ribs. A huge wolf stood looking down as it pulled a chunk for flesh from a body. He made a move for the weapon and grabbed it as he rolled. He was now facing the wolf. It looked up at him but kept its head low and growled. It was defending its food. Attoot shook the axe and screamed as loud as he could. The wolf growled louder as it bared its teeth. His blood ran cold as two other wolves came out from behind a house upon hearing their friend’s growls. Instinct forced Attoot to make a decision. He turned on his heels and ran. The wolves gave a half-hearted chase until he was far away from the bodies. The adrenaline that pulsed through Attoot's veins caused him to continue to run long after the wolves and given up chasing him.

He now found himself beyond the town’s walls in the surrounding fields. Further than he realised he had run from his house. He slowed down and walked for a while. The next village was half a morning’s walk.

As he walked he saw wisps of smoke rising a short distance away. Soon he could smell the wood burning on a campfire. He saw two men lay on the ground near the fire when an arrow zipped past his head. He set off running as another arrow skimmed his shoulder. He pressed his hand to the wound as blood oozed between his fingers. The sound of someone running came from behind him, then a searing pain flashed across his lower back. He stumbled and came to a halt, looked down and saw the head of an arrow protruding from his belly. He turned and saw an ugly man running at him. He realised his adversaries were goblin men. As the goblin got close it raised its axe and screamed. Attoot stepped aside and swung his axe at head height. He felt it bite, and the goblin’s body took one more step before its legs collapsed beneath it and it crashed to the ground. Its head bounced and rolled across the moss covered earth before coming to a standstill on its left ear. The eyes with their dark green sclera looked up at Attoot and the horrible lips twitched a little as if trying to form words. Another goblin was already running at Attoot. As it reached him their axes clashed. They attacked each other with matching ferocity. Blocking and attacking each other over and over. Until Attoot knocked the goblin's axe aside and hacked off its right arm. He turned the axe, brought it back and sliced off its left leg. It fell to the ground, and he buried the head of his axe into its heart, killing it instantly. The last goblin threw down its weapons and raised its hands to show it was unarmed. It forced an awkward smile onto its face, then turned and ran. Atoot considered chasing it but knew with the arrow in him he wouldn't be able to run fast enough. Beside that, he had to continue his journey. The arrow in his belly made walking to the next village all the more difficult. He was driven on by the need to warn the people there and to return with help for Marriat, Valetice and any other survivors.

After what felt like hours, he reached the gate in the walls of the village called Ghodersvac. His breathing was becoming laboured, and his legs were growing heavy. Two guards, Bord and Tarc, were stood at its open door.

"Help me, please!" he called.

The guards saw him as he stumbled towards them.

"What happened to you?" said one of the guards.

"My village has been attacked by a dragon," said Attoot.

He then stumbled and Bord quickly moved towards him as he fell to the ground.

"Tarc, help me get him inside," said Bord.

Tarc was already running to his aid. They picked him up and carried him into Ghodersvac village square.

Ghodersvac was made up of a central hall and twenty houses, all surrounded by a tall wooden wall. There was a blacksmith, bakers, butchers, story sellers and healer all within the walls.

"Dienco! Lord Dienco!" Tarc yelled.

A huge man with long, black hair, and a large, bushy, grey beard stepped out of the hall and strode towards them.

"Yes, why do you call for me?" he said. His voice deep and noble.

"This traveller has just arrived at our door. He's injured. Says his village has been attacked by a dragon," said Tarc.

"Bring him over here and put him on the slab," said Dienco.

They carried him over and lay him down on the huge slab of stone that stood infront of the hall. Dienco put his hand on Bord's shoulder.

"Fetch Skalat," he said.

"Yes Lord," said Bord and ran to the healer's house.

"What's your name, son?" said Dienco.

"Attoot. I'm from Aslakvaas."

"What happened to you?" said Dienco.

"The town was attacked early yesterday. It was a dragon, but like none I have ever seen before. Small for a dragon and shaped like a man, but still a lot taller than any man. It attacked people, they changed and attacked other people. I ran to my wife and her brother. They work as bakers, but they were running towards me. We made it to our house and barricaded the door. We could hear the screams from other people getting torn apart outside. Eventually it all went quiet. We were scared to move until the sun rose this morning. Everyone else is dead. It was up to me to warn people, that thing is still out there. Their bodies are still strewn around the village. They're attracting wolves and other wild things. Please, help my wife and her brother. They are still there. The lands between our villages are too dangerous for us all to have travelled," said Attoot.

"Is that where you got the arrow? Making your way here?" said Dienco.

"Yes. I was attacked by goblin men. I killed two with my axe and the third ran. I could not chase it. I already had the arrow in me by then," said Attoot.

"The gods must be watching over you. Goblins don't usually miss a kill. Hmm, Ok. Let's get that arrow out of you. This is going to hurt a lot. Lads hold him down," said Dienco.

Four men held down Attoot's limbs and Dienco was about to grab the arrow to break off the tail end off it, when a shout stopped him short.

"Don't touch it!"

An old man hunched over a walking stick approached them. He wore a hooded cloak with bottles, trinkets and charms attached to his belt.

"Why not?" said Dienco.

The old man walked over to the stone slab and stood at Dienco's side. He touched his finger to the head of the arrow, then to his tongue and spat. His face curled up in a grimace.

"This is Skalat, our healer," Dienco said to Attoot.

"Faderot," said Skalat.

"What is Faderot?" said Attoot.

"It's a poison made from Fade root fungus. It acts fast. The goblins use it because they're the only thing it won't kill," said Skalat.

"What do you mean, the only thing it won't kill? Is there a cure? There has to be a cure," said Attoot, he clenched his teeth and tears welled in his eyes.

"Sorry, my boy, you're not going to survive. The only thing we can do is get that arrow out and dress the wound. You're lucky to have made it this far," said Skalat, with a pained expression on his face.
A rush of panic shot through Attoot. He grabbed Dienco's arm.

"Don't pull the arrow out. Please find my wife, Marriat, and her brother, Valtice. Get them somewhere safe," he said.
Then his whole body stiffened, his jaws clenched together, and four heavy breaths rasped through his teeth. His head fell, slack and heavy onto the stone slab, and he was dead.
Dienco put his hand to the man's face and closed the eyelids. He lowered his head for a moment. He let out a long breath, then looked up at the people of his village.

"This man gave his life to get here and warn us of an imminent danger. A danger that killed his whole village except for him, his wife and his brother. His name was Attoot. Now he lies dead. We will honour him. Brogen, make sure he has a proper funeral. Talish, write a song of his courage. I need all the men who are of fighting age and health to follow me to his village and bring his wife back here. There have been sightings of a dragon in these lands for at least one full moon. Our village is not safe anymore," he said.

"We should go, find this beast, and slay it," said Tarc.

"Yes, it could be us next. We should act now!" said Bord.

"But we could lose all our men. If that thing can kill a whole village, it could kill all of us too," said a thin man with wispy hair on his old face.
The crowd began to mutter among themselves. Dienco raised his fist into the air and they were

silenced at once.

"We cannot just wait here and hope it does not come for us. We need to attack. Not only to save our village but to protect this land," said Dienco.

"I treated Ruhsarr Miehyelzah at his farm just outside Aslakvaas four days ago. He was attacked by the dragon, but somehow, he survived. He had sustained grave injuries, but he is strong and was fighting the wounds" said Skalat.

"I know the man you of whom you speak. Ruhsarr son of Anzo. I hear he has slain dragons before. We should find him. He will be able to help us take on the beast," said Dienco.

"But he's injured. How can he help us?" said the old man.

"You just heard the healer. He says his wounds are healing. Even if he can't help us fight maybe he can help us with knowledge," said Dienco.

"Why are we standing here talking? Let's get on with it!" said a huge man, shaking his heavy axe in the air.

"All who are willing to take on this beast say aye," said Dienco.

Nearly every person said, "Aye!"

"It is decided. We set out at noon. We'll attack under the cover of darkness and surprise the beast. Arm yourselves and say farewell to your loved ones for some of us may not return. But know this, a death by a dragon is an honourable and proud death!" said Dienco. "Ready yourselves and drink deep for tonight we hunt a dragon!"

They people cheered then headed off to their homes to retrieve their weapons and say goodbye to their families. They all uttered promises of their victorious return. Promises, that for some of them, would become lies. In their haste, none of them noticed the winged being that flew high above and listened to their plans.

"Oh, you fools. You will not find the man, Ruhsarr. The Dragon Lord Ruhsarr will have a surprise waiting for you, though," he said with a smile.

He then changed direction and flew back towards his cave to make his plans.

Chapter 27.

By the time the group of Ghodersvacian villagers reached Aslakvaas it was early afternoon. The bodies of the vampire attack victims still lay where they had fallen. Some had already begun to putrefy, and the smell drew animals and insects that now fed on them. Some had almost been picked clean. The bodies of Theda and a few others were completely gone. The sun was still high in the sky but had already begun its steady descent towards the horizon.

Tarc lit a fire, and the others lit torches off it. They used them to chase away the animals. When they were certain that they were safe from attack they searched the houses. After a few minutes of searching someone called out,

"Lord Dienco, this house here, the door is barricaded from inside."

Dienco came running to the long house.

"Marriat, Valetice?" he said as he banged on the door.

There was the noise of someone scrabbling about inside as they removed the barricade and opened the door slightly.

"Who are you? What do you want?" said Marriat. She had only opened the door enough for Dienco to see one of her eyes through the gap.

"My name is Dienco. My warriors and I are from Ghodersvac. Your husband, Attoot, sent me to find you."

"Is he here with you? Attoot, is he here?" said Marriat, as she opened the door a little more.

"M'lady your husband had the strength of a bull, and an iron will. He fought wolves and goblins to reach our village. Unfortunately, the goblins pierced him with a Faderot poisoned arrow. He fought on to find our village and our help, sadly the Faderot took hold. His last words were of you. He told me to save you," said Dienco.

Marriat stepped back and fell to her knees sobbing.

"Attoot! My Attoot! You have been stolen from me!" she cried.

Dienco pushed opened the door just enough that he could see the woman through the opening.

"Your husband was an honourable and courageous man. Please let us take you back to our village where you will be safe."

He held out his hand. She hesitated for a moment but then looked into his eyes and saw the sincerity there. She took his hand then and he helped her to her feet.

"This is Tyron and Raimi. They will escort the two of you back to Ghodersvac. They are strong and able warriors," said Dienco.

"I want to come with you," said Valetice.

"You are to go with your sister to protect her," said Dienco.

"I am able to fight and can handle myself. I am twelve years old and nearly a man," said Valetice.

"We need men who have seen many more winters. It will be dangerous and Attoot sacrificed his own life to find us to help you. Do not let his death be in vain. Go with your sister, she has lost too much already this day," said Dienco.

Valetice was reluctant but he too looked into Dienco's eyes. He saw wisdom there and nodded his head.

"I understand," he said.

"Good lad. Now go before it gets too late. There are still more than a few hours till the sun goes down, but you do not want to be out here when the darkness falls," said Dienco.

"Ok, thank you. May the gods guide your axes,"

said Marriat.

"And may they grant you safe passage back to my village," said Dienco.

Marriat, Valetice, Tyron and Raimi gathered their things and set off back to Ghodersvac.

Dienco whistled and his people gathered together.

"We have to clean this place up. The bodies are drawing beasts of all kinds. There isn't enough time to burn each body separately, so we are going to burn them all together. Gather up all the wood you can and we'll make a pyre in the square," said Dienco.

They gathered up all the wood they could find then collected the bodies and placed them all on top of the pile. It was tough work, but it was necessary.

An hour later they all stood round the wooden pyre with their torches held high.

"These people all fell to the beast. May they find peace in the afterlife, and may their spirits aid us in the finding and destroying of this beast. It is a curse on our land, and the duty has fallen to us, the people of Ghodersvac, to rid our land of its presence," said Dienco.

With that they all held their torches to the pyre until the fire took hold. Soon the flames engulfed it and all the bodies upon it.

"Our work here is done. It is time to find Ruhsarr. Pick up your belongings and we'll get moving," he said.

"Aye," they all said.

They walked out through the town gates.

"According to directions Skalat gave me Ruhsarr's house is on the edge of the forest furthest from the sunset," said Dienco.

Chapter 28.

By the time the Miehyelzah farmhouse came into view the groups shadows were growing long. It was nestled on the outskirts of the forest. Soon they were close and could see that the door was lit by the warm glow of a fire.

Dienco approached the house and thumped on the door with his huge hand. It was opened by a tall, brunette woman. He was struck by her beauty and rendered speechless, something that had never happened to him before. She had a fierce look in her eye and held a spear in her right hand.

"What is the meaning of this? Who are you and why are you banging on my door as the sun sets? Don't you know that dangers lurk here in the night?" She demanded while she held the spear in a threatening manner.

"B-B-Begging your pardon M'lady. We're from Ghodersvac village across the valley. We heard about the attack in Aslakvaas. We were told it was the work of a beast," said Dienco.

"Yes," her fierce expression softened a little. "It was a great shame. I knew some of the people who were killed. That still doesn't answer my question of why you are here!" said the woman.

"We're on a quest to slay the beast who committed the attack. We are looking for Ruhsarr to ask for his help. It is said that he has dealt with dragons before," said Dienco.

"You're right, he has. He is not here right now. He went to fetch firewood. You're welcome to come in and wait for him. He shouldn't be too long. I've made a stew if you are hungry," said the woman.

"Very gracious of you M'lady. The road has been long and strenuous," said Dienco.

"Place your weapons by the door. Forgive me for

coming across as accusatory but I don't know you and I'm a woman alone in her home," she said.

"Of course, M'lady," said Dienco. "Down your weapons at the door, people," said Dienco.

As the group walked into the house, they left their weapons on the ground, then took a seat by the fire.

"Begging your pardon M'lady," said Bord. "Are you a relation of Ruhsarr? I thought his wife had blonde hair."

"Theda was killed a year ago. It was very sad. I'm Gilad, Ruhsarr's new wife."

"May I ask how she died?" said Bord.

"Oh, she bled to death. An accident with a blade. Working these fields can be dangerous. It was very sad," she said.

"That is very unfortunate. You have my condolences. My family knew her family, but I had not seen her for years," said Bord.

"Who wants stew?" said Gilad, changing the subject.

All the group said, "Yes please."

"I just need to pass water first," said Tarc and got to his feet.

"Keep your eyes open, the night draws in," said Dienco.

"Will do," said Tarc.

He smiled and nodded at Gilad and walked to the door and stepped outside.

He walked away from the house trying to get out of earshot of the people inside. He found some long grass, walked into it, and began to do his business. Something rustled behind him.

"Yes, very funny," he said.

The rustling continued, so he finished urinating, pulled up his pants and turned round.

"I said very fu..."

The words stuck in his throat as he found himself

looking at the huge head of a hairless, scale-covered beast. Its big, orange eyes were stone cold and looked right into his. He opened his mouth but before he could make another sound a huge hand wrapped around his throat and squeezed. He was then lifted off his feet. His eyes bulged in terror and the little capillaries across their surfaces began to burst. The beast lifted him to its mouth and its long, serrated teeth bit into his head. They sank into the flesh below his ears with ease and there was an audible pop as Tarc's skull collapsed under the pressure. With a jerk of his neck Ruhsarr tore most of the man's head from the body. He chewed the skull, crunching the bones with little resistance, and swallowed. He then drank the blood from the shredded flesh that had moments ago been Tarc's lower face and cast the body aside.

"Where on earth is he? He only went to piss!" said Dienco.
A concerning amount of time had passed and Tarc had still not returned. He looked to Gilad, but she just shrugged her shoulders and gave a sly smile. Dienco realised that something was amiss.
"What is this? I want to know where he is!" he said.
"Our master has dealt with him," said two female voices from the stables in the next room.
"Your master? Who is in there? Come out at once!" said Dienco.
Two women walked into the room where the light of the fire made their snow white faces glow. All the people looked at them and got to their feet. Some of them smiled for a moment but their smiles soon turned to frowns and expressions of worry and fear. Something about the way these women moved, and their posture wasn't right.

“No Ruhsarr, and now women hiding in the stables? I demand to know what is going on here!” said Dienco.
Gilad spoke but not in to answer Dienco’s question.
“Feed on them but don’t kill them. The master wants to turn them into his warriors.”
The women began to move closer to the group. Gilad opened her mouth wide and hissed as her eyes turned flame yellow. Her cheekbones and eye sockets became pronounced from her face. Her skin puckered and turned to scales and all her teeth elongated into fangs. The people began to scream. She reached out and attached herself to the nearest person and tore a chunk of flesh from his neck. A similar transformation overtook the two women who then threw themselves into the group and began to bite whoever was nearest to them. The people tried to fight off the blood thirsty attackers, but they moved too fast and were far too strong. One man ran for the door just as it burst in. He was thrown back into the crowd. Two huge arms ripped the doorframe up from its moorings and took a large area of the roof with it. The beast then smashed the walls on either side to widen the space. Dienco looked to the hole that had been torn in the building. He saw what looked somewhat like a dragon, somewhat like a giant man. It was partially silhouetted against the moon and partially lit by the fire. The light flared in its eyes. He stumbled back and tripped over one of his people. He looked round and saw most of them lay on the floor with their necks torn open. The women were still biting and lapping at blood that pumped from torn flesh. Some writhed on the floor as others got to their feet. He looked back at the dragon as it stepped menacingly towards him. Irt hunched over so it could look him in the eyes. A grin spread across its almost human

face as its breath rasped between its blood encrusted teeth.

"What are you?" he said, his voice unsteady and hoarse.

It smiled even wider as it drew closer, carefully stepping between the bodies without breaking eye contact until it stood directly in front of Dienco. It then spoke in a deep, rumbling hiss of a voice.

"I am whom you seek, Dienco. You are in my house."

"Ruhsarr?" Dienco said in a whisper.

Ruhsarr reached down, grabbed him by the chest and lifted him to his open mouth. Dienco punched him in the face but received a laugh for his feeble effort. In a moment he was lifted in close, and in spite of all his struggling and all his strength, Ruhsarr sunk teeth into his throat. Enough blood was drained to weaken but not kill him. Ruhsarr placed the limp body of Dienco on the floor and watched as he began to change. He pulled himself to his feet and stumbled about for a moment before he regained his balance. He began to claw at his face and screamed as long spinney teeth pushed their way out through his gums. He then opened his eyes. They had changed to an intense blue with almond shaped pupils. He looked at Ruhsarr, where before he had seen him as a beast, he now saw him as God-like and his new master.

Ruhsarr looked at him and the group of newly created vampires as they stood before him. They gazed back at him with admiration and adoration in their eyes. Taking in the sight of this new being with a sense of amazement and wonder.

"Kneel before me," he said.

All in the room dropped to their knees.

"Dienco, I have many plans for you. You were a natural leader, now you are much more than that. I have a great gift to bestow upon you, and in return I want you to lead my army," he said as he drummed his fingers on the skin that sealed the huge vase.

"This is the life blood of the dragon you sought. The dragon who made me what I am, and the dragon I slew. Drink from this vase. You will drink in the dragon's power, and you will be reborn."

He removed the skin from the vase and beckoned Dienco over. The new, tall, bearded vampire got to his feet and approached the vase with some hesitation. He looked down into the mouth of the vessel. Inside he saw the deep red liquid. He looked back up at his new Lord.

"Drink, my child," said Ruhsarr with a smile.

Dienco lowered his hands into the liquid and cupped them together, then lifted them to his mouth. It was thicker than human blood and clung to his skin like honey. He poured it into his mouth and swallowed, then licked the remnants from his hands. Nothing happened. He dipped his hands in again and drank but there was still no effect. He went to drink again but the power of the blood hit him harder than any mead he had ever drank. A surge of energy pulsed through every cell of his body, his throat burned and his head span. His vision went dark, his hearing faded out and he thought he was going to pass out. He stumbled but maintained his balance. After a few seconds of swaying back and forth his vision and hearing returned with a clarity the like of which he had never experienced. Everything about him felt like it had been improved. His thoughts were faster, and his hearing exquisite. He looked out through the hole where the door had been into the night beyond. Where he should have seen darkness he now saw the fields and trees as if he was seeing them in the daytime. The power coursed through him. He threw his head back and let out a deep thunderous roar as his body grew in every aspect. His muscles strained against the seams of his clothes. Streaks of red emanated out from his pupils and into his iris'. They gleamed with his newly acquired strength.

"Ruhsarr, my Lord, build your army and I will lead it. All life will bow to you, and the gods will envy your power. I am yours to command, my master," his voice boomed like thunder.

"Yes they will," said Ruhsarr.

He smiled as he slapped a hand on Dienco's shoulder, and his vampires bowed down in praise of him.

Chapter 29.

The next night Ruhsarr released his followers into the night.

"Go my children. Quench your thirst, but return before the sunrises," he said.

Dienco and the others filed out of the building. A few of them scampered off in pack but Dienco strode back and forth for a few moments. His legs buzzed and his body twitched with energy. He was overcome with the need to run. He stopped pacing, looked out into the night and sped off into the darkness in a full sprint. Over fields and foothills, moving faster and faster with every stride. He dodged trees and jumped over cows. A bear roared at him from the forest and birds scattered from their roosting places.

A scent caught his nostrils then. The scent of human blood. He followed it and was led to a homestead at the foot of a mountain a short way from a village he didn't recognise. He approached silently. He opened the door and creeped inside, not even thinking about who could be in there. Beside a small fire a woman lay on the ground covered in furs and pelts. The man beside her sat up and looked up at him but in the dying embers of the fire all his human eyes saw was a vague silhouette in the dark. Before he could even make a sound Dienco was on him and biting deep into his neck. The blood pumped furiously from the wound and spilt down his chin and across his face. He bit down harder and sealed his mouth around the wound. The gasps and hollow coughs from the man's lungs stop and the empty body lay limp in Dienco's arms. He cast it aside and the woman stirred. Swift and silent, Dienco moved into the corner and watched her.

"Ecore? Ecore, I think someone is in here. Ecore?

Wake up!" she said.
He could hear the panic growing in her voice. She began to feel around the room and her hand found the man's limp body. She let out a soft whimper. Dienco found that he enjoyed the sounds she made. He found her fear delicious.

"Ecore? What is wrong with you?"
Dienco growled from his hiding place and the woman screamed. He pounced on her and pinned her down. She wailed and he revelled in it.

"There is no Ecore here," he hissed.
The scream began to erupt from her mouth, but his teeth sank into her neck. Hot blood pulsed from the wound and her screams died just before her heart beat for the final time. With her the last vestiges of humanity within Dienco died too. The blood twisted his thoughts. Any love he had for humans was gone. He held no more respect for humans than they would have for vermin.

Chapter 30.

Over the following days Ruhsarr spent most of his time flying among the clouds. He scanned the landscape with his advanced sight. He could pick out individual people and their body heat. There were little groups of houses, homesteads, and farms. He wanted more than this. Soon he found exactly what he was searching for. It was a large town with a fortified outer wall of wood and stone. It was fifteen feet high and six feet thick at the bottom. There was a tower in the middle that stood twenty five feet tall. He flew over it and looked at the other buildings within the perimeter. There was a blacksmith, a carpenter, a stone mason, a brickmaker and a ropemaker. A healer and herbalists, bonesetters. A butcher, baker, and fish merchants. He looked at the number of houses and estimated there must be a population around two hundred people. Over twice the population of Aslakvaas. He assumed that the tower must be home to a Chieftain or Lord. This fortification was built to defend against attacks from other humans on the ground. Dragons were at the top of the food chain. Their attacks came from the air, were rare, and usually fire based. There was very little the humans had in the way of defence against such a superior beast. Large bows and arrows with weighted ropes, and spears used in an attempt to bring the animal down were the height of their technology. Ruhsarr smiled to himself. With him being so much smaller than even the smallest of dragons he could easily navigate around these defences. He was a new species. They would not know how to stop him and his minions, or if he could even be stopped.

He flew back to his home where all the other vampires had been hiding out. He walked through the door and Dienco ran towards him.

"Your people are hungry. When are you going to let us out again. We can't take much more of this. Please Lord Ruhsarr!" he said.

"I know my child, we all are. Hold on just a little longer," said Ruhsarr.

"How much longer? Please say tonight," said Dienco who was nearly grovelling on his knees now.

"Tonight, as the sun sets," said Ruhsarr.

"Oh, thank you Lord! What do you have planned, kind sir," said Dienco.

"Tonight, we travel to the place I have spent days searching for. There we will all feed our hunger until our bellies are fit to burst. From those we feed upon I will build my army," said Ruhsarr with a smile.

Soon the hour was upon them. The sun had settled down beyond the horizon and the narrow slit of the crescent moon had risen and was low in the night sky. Ruhsarr and his people moved out from the Miehyelzah farmhouse under the cover of darkness. Moving with their newfound speed they covered the distance faster than any human could, even if they were on horseback. They approached the town in complete silence.

"Stay here. You will know when I am ready for you," said Ruhsarr.

"Yes, my Lord," said Dienco.

A man patrolled the top of the walls of Fallohade town. He looked out onto the dark land beyond the walls. He saw an area of ground undulate in the thin moonlight as if it was moving toward the wall. He called to another man who looked over to him.

"Jar. What is that? I think I see people down there. maybe twenty of them moving this way," he said.

"Knowing you, Gres, it's probably just a herd of goats again," said Jar from further up the wall. At that moment they both heard something fly swiftly overhead. Gres looked up but saw only stars and clouds. A croak came from Jar's direction. Gres looked over to his friend but saw a large figure moving at a fast pace along the wall towards him. He raised his bow, aimed and loosed an arrow at the thing. It stuck into the surface flesh of the Ruhsarr's chest. He swept it away like a man swatting a mosquito. He reached out a hand and clenched it tight around Gres' throat, lifted him from the wall and threw him over the outer side. Dienco jumped on him the moment he hit the earth and bit into his neck. A burning pain surged through his body and he began to convulse.

Ruhsarr leapt from the wall and landed inside its perimeter beside two men stood by the gates. He grabbed one and quickly broke his neck with a flick of his wrist. As the other guard turned to see what was going on Ruhsarr lifted him by the shoulders and bit into his neck. The man began to convulse as he was dropped to the ground. Ruhsarr turned to the gates and examined them. They were in the shape of an arch, and both tall and wide enough to allow a horse drawn sled to pass through with ease. There was a huge wooden beam across the middle bracing them shut. He took it with both hands and lifted it away with ease as a group of guards ran up behind him. They shouted as they shook their weapons at him and shot arrows into his back. He turned and swung the timber like a giant bat, and struck three of them. The impact knocked them off their feet and shattered their bones. One lay dead, while the other two lay in the mud with bones protruding from their limbs that sat at awkward angles. For their trouble when they tried to breathe but could only cough up blood. The one guard who was left standing turned to run but Ruhsarr threw the timber at him like a spear. It caught him in the back of the head and forced his face deep into a nearby wall.

Ruhsarr turned and pulled open the gates. His followers, led by Dienco, flooded into the town like a plague. They attacked the people they found in the streets. They tore their way into the homes and attacked the people inside. Screams rang out from every house they entered. The town quickly fell into a state of chaos. Guards and armed townspeople attacked Ruhsarr. He moved through them, calmly broke their limbs, drained them of blood and cast them aside as he went. Soon there was a large trail or bodies behind him. They began to get to their feet as they were transformed by the violation that mixed with their blood. Ruhsarr called to all his followers. They turned and looked towards him with blood and flesh hanging from their mouths.

“Turn every human you find. I want every last one of them. I'm going to the tower,” he growled.

All of the followers, old and new, moved through the town and continued their trail of destruction and assimilation. Ruhsarr turned more people and guards as he went. When he arrived at the tower he was impressed but its size and construction. It had a square foundation and loomed menacingly over him. The door opened and five men stepped through it. They lined up infront of the building and he noticed they weren't dressed in the same clothes as the rest of the guards. Two were clothed in buffalo skins, and two were clothed in wolf skins. The last one out, who now stood in the middle, was clothed in a bear skin. He was larger than the others and at least a head taller. He reminded Ruhsarr of his human self. He stepped forwards.

“Stay back beast. You go no further,” he said.

"Step aside. I come to claim this fortress for my own. You can surrender to me or suffer the same fate as your guards at the front gate," said Ruhsarr, his teeth still stained red with blood.

The man pointed his axe at Ruhsarr.

"I am Henru, the Lord of Fallohade town. Sworn protector of this town and its people. I'll tell you what is going to happen. You are going to leave here and take all your monsters with you. If you refuse, it is you who will die."

"Ah, the Lord of Fallohade you say. Then it is you I am here to see. Once again I extend my offer. Surrender or die."

"I've heard enough," said Henru.

He lunged towards Ruhsarr, and his axe sliced the air. With hardly any effort Ruhsarr dodged the weapon. Henru landed and quickly turned to face Ruhsarr, who took a step towards him. He opened his mouth and bellowed out a confidence shattering roar.

"Shout all you like, you don't scare me, beast," said Henru.

Ruhsarr swung a clawed hand, but Henru was a well trained axeman. With a swift move of his weapon he cut off the hand. Ruhsarr let out a pained howl. Henru stepped in and slashed his thighs, splitting the flesh down to the bone. Blood poured from the wounds and Ruhsarr fell to his knees.

"Do you yield beast?" said Henru.

Ruhsarr looked him in the eyes and smiled. The wounds on his legs stopped bleeding and the flesh pulled back together and healed in a matter of seconds. He got back to his feet and raised his arm. Spikes of bone grew out from the stump where his limb had been sliced off. They formed the bones of the wrist. Strands of muscle grew like tentacles. They weaved side to side until they found the bones and attached themselves to it in layers. From the wrist, the bones of the hand formed, and then the fingers. Finally, skin and scales covered the whole thing. It was a new arm and identical in every way to the one he had lost. He clenched his new hand into a fist.

"Looks like I'll have to try harder," said Henru.

A crowd gathered around the base of the tower. There were no humans among them. Ruhsarr strode towards Henru who leapt aside and slashed him across the shoulder. Ruhsarr spun around. As he did Henru swung the axe down heavily and buried the head in Ruhsarr's chest. He wrenched the handle and tried to work the axe free, but it was stuck. Ruhsarr grabbed him by the throat. He continued to pull at the axe, but Ruhsarr knocked his hands away. He lifted Henru off the ground then pulled the axe out with his free hand and dropped it. It hit the ground with a heavy thud. He held the man closer to his face and opened his mouth wide bearing his gore drenched teeth. They were inches away from Henru's neck. He suddenly slammed his jaw shut and grimaced in pain. He looked around and saw the man in the buffalo skin had thrust a spear into his side. He threw Henru against the tower wall and drove his elbow into the buffalo man's head. Henru landed heavily and slumped to the ground. The buffalo man stumbled around for a moment. The left side of his head had collapsed. The pressure had forced his eyes from their sockets and grey brain matter oozed from a split in his forehead. The three other men ran at him. He grabbed one by the scruff of his neck and simply threw him into the crowd. The followers jumped on him. In seconds he was drained of blood and beginning to turn. Ruhsarr delivered a kick to the next man's groin and launched him into the air. He caught him by the ankle and swung him like a rag doll into the third man who was knocked into the crowd. He suffered the same fate as the other man. Ruhsarr then held up the man he had by the ankle. He took hold of his waist, turned him the right way up, and sunk his teeth deep into the neck. He too was then thrown into the crowd. Ruhsarr turned his attention back to Henru. He picked him up and tried to make him stand, but is legs hung limp from his waist and couldn't take his weight. Ruhsarr held him against the wall.

"Will you join me now?" he said.

"I have already given you my answer." said Henru.

His words slurred as blood poured from his quivering lips.

"I know you're hurt. I can make all your pain go away. All you need to do is join me. You could be a great leader in my army," said Ruhsarr, there was pity in his tone.

"You could ask until the skies fall. I will never join your army of monsters," Henru said as he glared out into the crowd of faces of people he once knew.

Ruhsarr tried to speak in a more persuasive tone.

"We could rule these lands..."

Henru spat a bloody glob of phlegm into his face. He recoiled in disgust for a moment and then reopened his eyes.

"So be it! You have chosen death!" said Ruhsarr. He slammed Henru down onto the stone floor and rolled him over on to his chest. He pushed the claws of his hand into the flesh of the man's back and took hold of his spine. He then tore out a fist full of vertebrae and cast them aside. He pushed his hand through the gap in Henru's spine and into his chest. He wrapped his fingers around the beating heart and pulled it until the veins and arteries snapped. Henru would have screamed but the only sound he could manage was a moan that seeped from his bloody lips. Ruhsarr grabbed Henru by the head, dug his claws into the bone and twisted it. With a rip, a crunch, and spurts of crimson blood, he tore it from the body. He held up the head and heart to the crowd. They roared a chorus of approval. He then dropped the heart into his mouth, swallowed it whole and roared back at the crowd.

"My children, my brothers and sisters, we are the new dawn. The reign of dragons and humans is over. The reign of vampires has begun. Nothing can stand in our way, all living things will bow to us. I will tear down the heavens and replace the old gods with one you can touch and see. I will be your god," he said with a wicked smile.

The crowd danced and cheered.

"Now pull this place apart. Turn all that you find. This is our town now!" he said.

With that he turned, stepped through the tower door and closed it behind him. Human screams and the roars of new vampires echoed from every building into the early hours of the morning.

Chapter 31.

Dawn broke over Fallohade town. The few vampires who were still outside scrabbled and ran into houses that had not been destroyed to escape the deadly sun. For all the carnage that had been bestowed upon the town in the night there were only a few dead bodies scattered around. The mission to turn as many humans as possible into vampires was a success. A long, metal spike had been attached to the top of the wall above the gates. Henru's head had been driven down onto it. The tip of the spike had pierced the top of his skull. His dead eyes were rolled back in their sockets, and his tongue hung loose from the mouth that hung open. The once great leader of the town had been reduced to a macabre warning to others that this was now a town of vampires. The new Lord of Fallohade was beginning to wake up in his tower.

Ruhsarr was feeling the immense power of all the blood he had consumed. He had drunk so much it made him feel inebriated. It pulsed through his veins and made his head spin. He opened his eyes and sat up. A dozen female vampires lay all around him on the bed. He surveyed them and smiled. As he reached out a hand towards one of them he saw that it was covered with the dark red of dried blood. He got to his feet and found that he was a little unsteady but managed to keep his balance. He stumbled to a chair, moved his wings to either side of it and sat down. It creaked under his weight but held. As he slouched forwards he lowered his head into his hands and placed his palms over his eyes.

In his mind's eye he saw a beautiful woman with blonde hair and green eyes. He realised she was Theda, his wife. The woman disappeared and was replaced by two figures. One was him as the human he used to be, and the other was the beast he had now become.

"By the gods, what have I done?" said the man. Images of Theda lay dead on the floor rushed through his mind like a nightmare.

"She tried to kill me!" said the beast.

"So you killed her? You, you butchered her," said the man.

"She got what she deserved! She opposed me!" said the beast.

"You tore her face off. I loved her yet you killed her. You're a monster!"

"A monster? Oh no, I am no monster. I am the most magnificent being that has ever lived!"

"You're a fiend, a murderer, and an abomination!"

"You may call me all the names you like, you snivelling wretch. You are a weak, pathetic human. I am the dawn of a new age, what man has always wanted to be. I am the Lord of a new species. The future of all life on this earth, and yet she opposed me! She…opposed…me! She deserved to die like all the others. All who oppose me will perish! I am Ruhsarr!" he said. With that the beast took the man by the throat and lifted him from the ground. His hand squeezed tight around the man's neck and his breath became a wheeze. "None will oppose me, not even you," said the beast as his hand clenched into a fist. He then gripped the head and tore it from the body. He squeezed it until the skull collapsed, and the brain spurt out from between his fingers.

Ruhsarr sat up and took in his surroundings. He tentatively got to his feet. The man he had been was gone forever and his transformation was complete. Humanity no longer defined him. He was neither man nor dragon, he was something even more powerful. Humans, even the ones he had known personally, were nothing more to him now than pray.

Chapter 32.

In the coming months Ruhsarr led his army to attack more villages and towns. The number of vampires grew from two hundred to six hundred. They used the same strategy that brought about their victory in Fallohade. With Ruhsarr initiating the attack then letting in the others to run amok within the town walls, turning the defences into a trap. Time moved on, and his army got even larger. The human inhabitants of the towns of Rogul, Afhek and Uapo abandoned their villages before Ruhsarr and his army even arrived. The people of Hurkotu, Alabba, and Lukkat surrendered without a fight. He offered them the same ultimatum that he had offered Henru, join me or die. He promised if they joined him, they would live forever. He didn't tell them they had to die and be transformed first, because of this vampirism was forced upon most people.

Chapter 33.

Dienco knocked on the wooden door of the stone tower in Fallohade. A guard opened a small window within the door and looked out at him.

"State your business," said the guard.

"I need to speak with Lord Ruhsarr," said Dienco.

"And you are?" said the guard.

"Master Dienco."

"Does Lord Ruhsarr know that you're coming?"

"No," said Dienco.

He swayed on his feet becoming frustrated.

"Then I am afraid. I can't let you in," said the guard.

"Gilo, this is the second time you have tried to keep me from entering the tower. I am Master Dienco. Leader of Lord Ruhsarr's army. I need to speak with him of important matters. Now open the door or I'll break it down," snarled Dienco.

Gilo realised his mistake and didn't hesitate. He slid the bolts aside and pulled open the heavy door. Dienco stepped through and strode towards Gilo who cowered down and away, trying to make himself as small as possible. Dienco pointed a finger at him.

"This is the second time you have opposed me. There will not be a third. Nod if you understand," said Dienco.

Gilo nodded and looked at his feet. Dienco hissed before he turned and strode away up the stairs.

He knocked on the door to Ruhsarr's throne room and a voice bellowed from inside.

"Enter."

He opened the door, stepped through, and found Ruhsarr with one arm folded over his chest and stroking his jaw with the other hand. He looked up at his guest.

"Ah, Dienco. My friend. What brings you here?"

"We seem to have some sort of dilemma, my Lord."

Ruhsarr smiled a little.

"Tell me more," he said.

"Hmmm, well. When you bit me, I changed. I bit my wife, and she changed. My wife bit her friend and that person died. People third down the line from you don't seem to be able to make new vampires. I worry that it will hinder our ability to increase our numbers. If the humans begin to group together and make bigger towns they will overwhelm us with ease. There was a group of travelling traders who passed through Ghodersvac a few years ago from lands where the sun is hotter. They told of a town so big it covered vast amounts of land. The amount of people there made all the people in the towns here look like a mere handful. Like a drop of water in a sea," said Dienco.

"That won't happen here. The farms would not sustain that many people. Also, the amount of people they have does not matter. They won't be able to stand against us," said Ruhsarr.

"Begging your pardon, my Lord, but you and a band of warriors were able to kill a dragon," said Dienco.

Ruhsarr stared at him for a few moments.

"Hmm. You're right. You have made a good argument. We will have to find out if there is some way to amend this problem. Thank you for bringing this to my attention," he said.

"You are welcome, my Lord," said Dienco.

"Is there anything else?" said Ruhsarr.

"No, my Lord," said Dienco.

"Sunrise is in less than an hour. I doubt you will make it back the Ghodersvac in time. You are welcome to stay here for the day, if you wish," said

Ruhsarr.

"I will be happy to be in your company, my Lord," said Dienco.

"Likewise," said Ruhsarr.

He smiled. He liked some of the vampires he had made, some he tolerated, and others he avoided at all costs. Dienco was different. He was a man after his own heart. He wanted control. To lead, to dominate, to snatch power from those he deemed unworthy of such strength. Sometimes he just wanted to enact despicable, unnameable, mindless violence and destruction. He knew Dienco would always have his back. He would never hinder him or stand in his way. He considered Dienco to be his true friend.

Chapter 34.

Five years into the expansion of this vampire empire, Dienco was in the courtyard in Ghodersvac training vampires to fight like soldiers when a messenger stepped out of the darkness.

"I seek Master Dienco. I have a message for him from Lord Ruhsarr," they said.

"I am Dienco. Out with it. What does he say?" said Dienco in a serious tone.

"You have been summoned to the home of Ruhsarr in the tower of Fallohade," said the messenger.

"Very well. Thank you. Tell him I am on my way," said Dienco more relaxed now.

He dismissed the soldiers and made his plans to travel that night.

Upon his arrival he went to the tower directly. As he entered the room, he saw Ruhsarr sat in a large backless throne. The naked and broken bodies of drained humans were strewn across the floor around the self-appointed god king.

"You wish to speak with me, my Lord," said Dienco.

"Yes, Dienco. As you are fully aware my army is growing. However, even with me as the great leader and you as my second in command it is expanding at a rate beyond our control of just the two of us. We need another layer of command between us and the soldiers. This will help us maintain control. I trust you as both a colonel and as a vampire. This is why I am giving you the responsibility to pick three more generals for my army. Do not worry, these generals will not supersede you. If fact they will answer to you as you answer to me. I will also dispense my orders to them through you. You have one month to find the candidates for these roles," said Ruhsarr.

"Very well my Lord. Are there any specific qualities you wish these candidates to display?" said Dienco.

"I want them to have abilities, physical or mental. Discerning abilities they will pass on to their offspring and therefore into the future vampire population," said Ruhsarr.

"As you wish my Lord," said Dienco, and bowed his head.

"Thank you, my friend. Fulfil this task for me. I know you will not disappoint me. You may leave now," said Ruhsarr.

"Yes, my Lord," said Dienco.

With that he bowed his head again and left.

*

The first place he went was the lavish village of Trusell. Here Gilad forced vampires who were under her spell to create extravagant items of clothing for her. Trinkets and jewellery cast in metals and carved from stone adorned her hands and neck. Beads were woven into intricately created dresses and tunics. Head scarves, shoes, undergarments, animal skins, furniture, cushions, blankets, and bedding were made all to her exact specifications. She would ask for beautiful things and her enchanted followers would make them for her.

Dienco approached her slowly in her home with a kind smile. She was fast and vicious and had a reputation of attacking anyone who so much as looked at her in a way she didn't like. Beside her a human was strung upside down by his feet. He was covered in wounds where she had bitten him and was slowly draining him. He was so far under her spell he believed this barbarism to be an act of love. He was lost in a delusion of ecstasy.

"Hello, Gilad," said Dienco.

She turned and looked at him and smiled. Her lips red with her victim's blood.

"Dienco, my brother, my lover, my friend. How are you?" she said.

She spun her words in a sensuous tone. They wrapped around Dienco's mind and drew him to her. The smile on his face grew into a look of adoration. She wrapped her arms around him and pulled herself close against him. He could feel himself falling under her spell. With a shake of his head he broke the illusion and looked at her with clear eyes. As strong as her spell was, the dragon's blood had reinforced his mind enough to allow him to slip out of her seductive spell. Without this strength it would be she who was sat in the throne at Fallohade with Ruhsarr and Dienco fulfilling her every whim.

"Lord Ruhsarr has sent me here with a task," he said.

"Really? What does our great leader require of me?" she purred.

She ran her fingers over his chest and slid her hand into his robes to caress the curve of his muscles.

"He wants me to fill the roles of three generals in his army," he said, trying to keep his mind on the assignment.

"And you thought of me?" she whispered, her lips inches from his.

Her fingertips caressing his skin.

"Erm, yes. You seem to possess the ability to control people's minds with little effort," he said and squeezed his eyes shut.

She slid a hand down between his legs. When she

felt no erection there, she stopped and smiled. She then uncoiled herself from him and pushed him away.

"You can resist me all you like. One day I will find a way into that mind of yours," she said.

"Maybe one day I will let you in. Right now, though, I have a task. Will you accept Lord Ruhsarr's offer? Your ability will be extremely useful to our kind," he said.

She looked him up and down.

"You want my ability, Gilad's gilamour? What is in it for me?" she said.

She turned back to the human. Bit into his thigh and swallowed a mouthful of blood.

"The only thing you love more than yourself, power," he said.

She looked at him and smiled.

"Dienco. you know me so well. I accept. Now will you stay a while. Have a drink with me," she said, that seductive tone back in her voice again.

"I will, but not from him," he said and grimaced a little.

"I have plenty of others. Bound or unbound? I know you like the hunt," she said.

A wicked smile played across his face.

"Give me an unbound one, with some fight in them," he said.

*

He travelled through the expanding vampire territories meeting with friends and new acquaintances. He met many new, strange, and interesting vampires. Many of whom had interesting abilities. Only a few though whose abilities were useful to him. To these he would reveal the task Lord Ruhsarr had set for him. He spoke with Bord after the successful raid of Garang, a small village in the east.

"You should meet with Saltorg. He's a spellcaster, and healer from Ornox," said Bord.

"Oh yes, the white hair in the weird village we captured a few moons ago," said Dienco.

"That's the one. He's the most talented healer I have ever met. Skarat is good, but Saltorg is amazing, the best. Better than the best," said Bord.

"Really, that good?" said Dienco, raising his eyebrows in exaggerated astonishment.

"Aye sir. He is the one you need to find. Trust me," said Bord.

"Where can I find this man?" said Dienco.

"I last saw him in Rellon. A small village one nights walk away. Not far from Fallohade. But, I have heard you won't need to find him. He finds the people who seek him. I don't know how he does it, but when he finds out you have spoken his name he will find you," said Bord.

His eyes were wide and with a hint of fear.

Dienco heard the name repeatedly over the next few days. Saltorg the Great, Saltorg the godhand, Saltorg the undying. His name proceeded him. It was clear he and this Saltorg definitely had to meet. He travelled through the towns looking for this elusive character.

He returned briefly to his home in Ghodersvac. He was awake making repairs to an inner wall when a tall, slender vampire with long, straight, grey hair and stern, piercing blue eyes walked into his house.

"I have heard that you seek me?" said this vampire.

Dienco looked at him with an air of confusion for a brief moment. Then he smiled and approached this new person in his home with his arms open wide.

"I presume you are the Saltorg that I have heard so

much about," said Dienco and clasped his hands on the man's shoulders.
Saltorg smiled suddenly and his expression was entirely transformed.

"Yes. That I am. I do hope that I am not intruding. I heard my name on the wind. You have been searching for me. I thought I would save you the hassle and I have found you," said Saltorg.

"That is very thoughtful of you. Do you know why I seek you?" said Dienco.

"No. I have not yet figured that out," said Saltorg.

"I have been told that you are the best healer, spellcaster in these lands," said Dienco.

"I also perform weapon blessings and cast the dark eye, for a price," said Saltorg with a smile.
Dienco then told him everything about Ruhsarr's task. Saltorg listened intently. When Dienco had finished Saltorg looked at him with those ice cold eyes, then bowed his head.

"It would be an honour," he said.
Dienco smiled at him.

"You have made the right decision. Our society will benefit greatly from your abilities. I will send word when I am ready for you to meet Lord Ruhsarr,"

"I will know," said Saltorg with a smile.

*

Dienco continued on his travels. He had a master of population control, a master of elements, and he was a master of war and hunting. Now he needed and master of agility and speed. He asked the vampires he met along the way if they knew of any incredibly agile vampires. He was pointed in the direction of a few individuals here and there, but none were exceptional. That was until he was pointed back toward Fallohade.

"There is a woman who can run faster than anyone I have ever seen there. She catches humans so fast they're dead before they even realise it," said a vampire he met in the street.

"What is her name?" said Dienco.

"You need to see the way she moves. Faster than the wind. Nature is no match for her. She bends as if her bones are made of rope," said another vampire he met.

"Her name, please? I must meet her," said Dienco.

"She calls herself Jorshean," the vampire replied.

He arrived in Fallohade Town a few hours later. He asked the people he met around the town and was directed towards the centre square. There a crowd had gathered to watch a performance. He was tall enough to see over their heads to a woman standing in the middle. She was talking to the people who had gathered around her.

"How high can you all jump? Higher than the roofs of the houses? Higher than the tallest trees?" she said.

"I can jump to the cliffs of Ulaf Slad," said someone in the crowd.

"Hmm, impressive. Although, I do believe that I can jump higher than any other vampire, with the exception of Lord Ruhsarr," said Jorshean.

She crouched down and her muscles tensed like coiled springs. Then she became a blur as her powerful legs were suddenly straight as they propelled her upwards. She continued her ascent, getting smaller and smaller the higher she went until she seemed to vanish even to Dienco's dragon blood enhanced eyes. Then she was coming down fast, hurtling towards the ground. As she fell she changed position. Flipping and rotating horizontally as she came down towards the ground. There was a thud as she landed that threw up a cloud of dust. As it cleared they could all see that she was kneeling down with her arms spread wide in a theatrical pose. The crowd applauded and shouted their approval. He waited for them to settle before she spoke again.

"Now, do we have any archers in the crowd?" she said.

Two people stepped forwards from the crowd. She handed then both a bow and a quiver of arrows.

"I want you to shoot arrows at me, and I want you to try to hit me. You won't be able to, but I want you to try," she said.

The two people shot arrows at her while she ran. She jumped and flipped over them and ducked under and dodged around them. She even caught some of them and slapped some of them out of the air. The crowd applauded and sang her name.

"Thank you, to these two lovely members of the crowd. Better luck next time. Now, my good people. I have one last trick. A show of speed," she said as she whisked a cover from a large cube that was revealed to be a cage. She unfastened the bindings on the front, lifted it, and beckoned to the human inside. The man shuffled forward cautiously. He stepped out and stood nervously in front of the crowd. Despite looking a little dishevelled he was healthy and well fed.

"Go on. Run," said Jorshean.

He looked around at the vampires that made up the crowd and then back at her.

"Go on. Run. You are free to go," she said.

His face twisted into an expression that seemed like he couldn't decide whether to laugh or cry. Then, he set off running as fast as he could. His legs pumped like engines. Jorshean and the crowd watched him. He was heading for the front gate and the world beyond the wall. The crowd and Dienco looked to

Jorshean, but she didn't appear worried. She pointed to the man and the crowed looked in his direction. There was a flurry of movement, then they all watched as Jorshean hit the man like a bolt of lightning. She lifted him from the grounds, and his legs were still cycling as she tore his neck open and lapped at the blood that spurt from the wound. His increased heartbeat forced the blood out at and even higher pressure than usual. She ran back to the crowd with the man, blood still arching from his neck. It cascaded over the crowd. Some ran from it giggling while others raised their hands and opened their mouths, like humans in the rain. The flow of blood slowed with the man's heart. When it was done the crowd burst into applause again. They chanted Jorshean's name while she held up the body an blew kisses to them.

When the show had ended, and the crowd had dispersed Dienco approached her.

"Your speed and agility are impressive," he said.

"Thank you, stranger," she said with a smile.

"My name is Dienco. I have an offer for you," he said.

"What kind of offer," she said, her expression tinged with suspicion and doubt.

"You say your abilities are only second to that of Lord Ruhsarr?" he said.

"That's right," she said.

"Why is that?" he said.

"Because he is my maker," she said.

"Ah, I am in good company then. He is my maker too," he said.

"Look, I'm busy I have another show to prepare for. What's the offer you spoke of?" she said.

"How would you like to prove yourself and perform for Lord Ruhsarr himself?" he said.

She smiled a little.

"You're serious?" she said.
"I am," he said.
"Then it would be and honour," she said.
"Good for you. I shall set up a meeting with him and call for you soon," he said. With that he went on his way to make the arrangements.

Chapter 35.

When the month had passed Dienco returned to Rusher's tower with the three candidates by his side. They entered the throne room and stood in a line patiently waiting for their Lord.

Ruhsarr strode in and took a seat in his backless chair. His huge wings hung down behind him unimpeded.

"Dienco. I see you have returned, and you are not alone. Does this mean that you have completed the task I set for you?" he said.

"Yes, my Lord. The task is complete, and I have brought you these three candidates. I believe they are the best vampires within your Kingdom, beside you obviously, my Lord. They all have specific attributes and abilities that I feel will greatly benefit the vampire bloodlines. I bring them here before you today seeking your approval," said Dienco.

"Very well, please present your candidates," said Ruhsarr.

"Yes, my Lord. The first candidate is Gilad," said Dienco. As he stepped aside, she stepped forwards. "You already know her, but she has some incredible abilities. She is beautiful, cunning and seductive. It gives her the ability to manipulate people both human and vampire into getting what she wants. She also has the ability to manipulate the shadows and the darkness so she can approach victims and enemies silently."

"Excellent. Ah yes, Gilad. We three are already acquainted. I am glad to see you hold no ill will towards each other," said Ruhsarr.

"Of course not, my Lord. I owe Gilad a debt of gratitude that I hope to repay with the position you will bestow upon her. Without her I would not be the vampire I am today," said Dienco.

Ruhsarr smiled with a smug expression.
"Who is your next candidate?" he said
"My next candidate is Saltorg," Gilad stepped back and Saltorg stepped forward and bowed his head. "He is a powerful warrior, healer, and spellcaster from the town of Ornox. He's been experimenting on himself and other vampires trying to make us more resilient to sunlight, fire and other weaknesses. In doing so he has elevated his own healing abilities," said Dienco.
"He is a good choice. We need people who can advance our abilities and reduce the effect of our weaknesses. Who is next?" said Ruhsarr.
"My last candidate is Jorshean," said Dienco. He invited her to step forwards as Saltorg stepped back. "She is the fastest and most agile vampire I have come across in my search. I have seen her jump a great height to the point she seemed to disappear, and she is so fast she can catch human's before they would even know she is hunting them. She can also disguise herself by changing her facial features at will," said Dienco..
"I am impressed. You have done well, Dienco. I approve of all these candidates. We should get started with the next stage of their vampiric improvement straight away," said Ruhsarr. He walked to the corner of the room, picked up the large vase, and carried it over to the centre of the room. He placed it in front of Dienco and the three candidates and removed the piece of material that covered the opening.
"Gilad, please step forward and drink."
She looked into the vase, and her eyes grew wide with awe.
"The dragon's blood," she said in a breathy whisper.
She was amazed that it was still liquid. Even now it

seemed more alive than any blood she had ever seen. Ruhsarr grinned at her. She bent down over the vase, dipped her hands into the blood then brought it up too her mouth and drank. She let out a strained gurgle, stumbled back and fell to her knees with her head bowed. Her face was wracked in a grimace.

"What's happening to her? What have you done?" said Jorshean.

"Just watch," said Dienco.

Gilad got back up to her feet and stumbled a little before she found her balance. She threw her head back and roared. Her muscles flexed as her body grew nearly a foot in height. She opened her eyes and Dienco saw they had light blue sclera with blood red irises.

"By the Gods, what is this?" said Jorshean.

"The life blood of a dragon. The ultimate and absolute power," said Ruhsarr with an evil smile. "Who will be next?"

Saltorg and Jorshean both stepped towards the vase at the same time and drank their fill. Their transformations began within them both at the same time.

Soon Ruhsarr smiled at the four improved vampires who stood before him.

"You have been changed by the dragon's blood. It has improved you physically and mentally in every way. Any abilities you had will be enhanced. You are elevated to generals within my army. You will answer to Dienco, he answers to me alone, and I answer to none. You are brothers and sisters bound by the same power that made me. The life blood of the dragon. From now on you will be known as 'The Children of the Blood," he said.

They all looked at him and then to each other. Each with a proud and vicious smile on their face.

Chapter 36.

The years passed and Ruhsarr continually proved himself to be a great but merciless Lord.

Since he and Dienco had spoken privately about the problem of third generation vampires not being able to turn humans it had become a widely known fact. The solution remained allusive but it by no means stop vampires from searching.

Most vampires had rooms or entire homes that let in no sunlight. Dienco and his wife, Khllet, were no different. One evening they opened the door to the blocked out room and stepped out.

"I am so hungry," said Dienco.

"We have plenty of stock. I rounded up a group last night while you were busy training the soldiers. Go and pick one," said Khllet.

"I knew I could smell the human stink. All their sweat and fear. Why do they always have to smell so bad?" he said.

He walked to the storeroom and opened the door. The animal smell wafted out towards him stronger now. Whines and whimpers came from within the room. He stepped inside. Three women and two men lay on the floor. Their wrists were bound to their ankles behind their backs with strips of leather. More wide strips of leather held cloths stuffed into their mouths, and covered their eyes, blindfolding them. They let out muffled groans and what might have been pleas for mercy when they heard him approach.

"Why must you keep them like this? You give them less respect than animals," he said to Khllet.

"They are so noisy and always try to escape or fight if they are not bound. Honestly, it's for their own good," she said.

He looked at her and raised an eyebrow.

"Ok. I also find the way they wiggle funny," she said with a hint of a smile.

"You find their attempts at movement funny? I think your reasons reach beyond humour. I think you enjoy seeing them stripped of mobility," he said.

"If you must know, I like the power I have over them. I mostly just find their wiggling funny," she said openly smiling now.

He watched them as they wiggled and strained so pathetically against their restraints. He had to admit, it was kind of funny.

"Well. Each to their own I suppose," he said.

He picked up one man and one woman by the cords that bound their wrist to their ankles and lifted them with ease. The two humans screamed into their gags as their limbs were wrenched back. He carried them out of the room and through to the living area, where he placed the woman down infront of Khllet. She looked at the woman and smiled the way someone does while looking at a steak. She knelt over the woman and bit into her neck lightly drawing a little blood. Unlike Dienco, who had to drain his humans before they began to change, she liked to savour the blood and sip at it. The woman thrashed her head around and the leather binding between her teeth came free. She spat out the cloth and before Khllet could react the woman lunged forwards and bit into her thigh, hard enough to draw blood and swallowed.

Khllet screamed and jumped to her feet, leaving the woman to fall back helplessly to the floor.

“What happened?” said Dienco, as he rushed to her side.

“She bit me. She, bit me,” she said.

The woman screamed and began to thrash and squirm. As the two vampires watched her, sharp teeth pushed out of her gums. She flexed her arms and the leather binding her wrists snapped. She kicked her legs out and freed her ankles. With a jerk of her body, she threw herself into the air and landed on her feet. She then launched herself at Khllet, who caught her by the throat.

“Dienco. What the fuck is happening to her?” said Khllet.

The woman continued to thrash and scream. She snapped her fanged jaws.

“You bit her, then she bit you?” he said.

“Yes. She bit me. Fucking bitch!” said Khllet.

“What have you done to me? What have you done?!” yelled the woman.

“Please. Try to relax. I’m trying to understand what has happened. You have just done something no one else has ever done,” he said.

“Let go of me, you fucking monster,” said the woman.

“If she let’s go of you, you have to stop trying to attack her,” he said.

The woman looked at him with so much hate and anger. Her eyebrows were furrowed as she bared her teeth. Then her expression softened.

“Ok. Ok,” she said.

She stopped thrashing and writhing and Khllet released her. Dienco took her by the shoulders and looked into her eyes. They were clear and the iris and sclera were a unified colour of grey. He took her by the hands and inspected her wrists. Where moments ago, there would have been scratches and burns from the leather there was now nothing but flawless unbroken skin. He continued to examine her fangs as he spoke to Khllet.

"I think the vampirism has spread from you to her through your blood. The same way Lord Ruhsarr spread the dragon's strengths on to Gilad, Saltorg, Jorshean, and me. The blood is the vessel, the key," said Dienco.

"She's a vampire?" said Khllet.

"It would seem so," Dienco said.

"A what?" said the woman.

"A vampire. One of us. You are no longer human. You will need to drink blood to survive the way we do. The thing is you are special. You are a new type of vampire," he said.

He proceeded to tell her about the vampire hierarchy and the problem with 3rd generation vampires not being able to turn humans.

"That is a lot to take in, and I'm so thirsty," she said.

Khllet led her over to the man who was still bound on the floor.

"Feed from him. The blood will ease your thirst and hunger," she said.

The woman driven on by her thirst bit into the man's neck and drank from him. She knelt back and licked her teeth.

"I feel so alive," she said.

"Let's try something. Feed him some of your blood," said Dienco.

He removed the gag from the man while the woman dug her nails into the palm of her hand. She then pressed her palm to his lips and let the blood fill his mouth. He shook his head and spat most of it away. Then he swallowed. He began to convulse, and fangs pushed from his gums as he arched his back and opened his mouth in a silent scream. He broke free of his bonds but was calm in comparison to the woman.

“What the fuck is going on?” he said sounding exhausted.

Dienco smiled and then laughed heartily.

“My new friend. We have just found out how to make more vampires. We must take you and,” He gestured towards the woman for her name.

“Unet,” she said.

“We will take Unet and you,” Dienco gestured towards the man.

“Collu.”

“We will take you, Unet, and you, Collu, to see Lord Ruhsarr. I’m sure Saltorg will be extremely interested to speak to you too,” said Dienco.

Chapter 37.

The next night they travelled to Saltorg's settlement in what was left of Aslakvaas. He had taken over the Elder's temple. Inside he had pulled down the stone circle and repurposed the stones into slabs that his subjects could lay upon as he administered his potions and poultices on and into their bodies. His subjects were selected from a group of followers he had made. Humans who he swore were all willing to be part of his experiments.

"Dienco. It's good to see you here in my little town.

"It's good to be here. Interesting what you have done with the place," said Dienco.

"Have you ever been here before, when it was a human settlement?" said Saltorg.

"I have been here to trade. This is the first time I have been in this building though. It seems strange being here again. It has a different atmosphere now that it is vampire orientated," said Dienco.

"We still have a human presence here in the day to rebuild the town. The human's do the more menial jobs and protect us by day, and we vampires move the heavier objects and protect the humans by night," said Saltorg.

"That is good. In Ghodersvac we have established a similar symbiotic relationship with the humans. Most of them we just kept as a food supply, but there a groups who have proven themselves to be trustworthy," said Dienco with a smile.

"I have given some of the humans here an incentive. Once every new moon I honour their hard work with one human being given the chance to become a vampire. In exchange for them allowing me to do my experiments on them," said Saltorg.

"What experiments are you working on that the moment?" said Dienco.

At that moment the sound of something large flying overhead reverberated through the building. There was a commotion, a voice screamed from outside, and then silence. The doors were pushed open and Ruhsarr walked in holding a man by his head. The body had been bitten, drained of all his blood, and was already limp.

"Lord Ruhsarr," said Dienco, Khllet and their two new vampires bowed their heads.

Saltorg stood and looked at the Lord in shock.

"What have you done to my guards?" he said.

"It was very kind of you to provide me with refreshments after my flight here," said Ruhsarr.

"Those were my guards. I have promised to protect them," said Saltorg.

"And very appreciated they were," said Ruhsarr.

"But," started Saltorg.

"They will be vampires now, they can protect themselves," said Ruhsarr and looked Saltorg in the eyes with a look that dared him to continue his protest. "Is there anything else, General Saltorg."

The lower ranking vampire swallowed his pride and disapproval.

"No, my Lord," he said eventually.

"Then show me my due respect," growled Ruhsarr.

Saltorg bowed his head.

"Lord Ruhsarr," he said in a clear tone without a single hint of malice.

Ruhsarr placed the body of the guard on the floor. The man went through the now recognised discomfort of vampiric transformation.

"So, are you going to tell me why I'm here, or do I have to guess?" said Ruhsarr.

"You might remember we talked a while ago about the 3rd generation not being able to turn humans," said Dienco.

"Yes. I remember," said Ruhsarr.

"Well, we think we may have solved that problem. This is Unet and Collu. A 4th and a 5th generation," said Dienco.

Ruhsarr's eyes widened.

"How is this possible?" he said.

"Khllet bit Unet to feed from her, then Unet attacked Khllet and bit her. After that Unet turned. Unet then bit Collu and fed him some of her blood and he also turned. We thought that it might work in the same way as the dragon's blood. That is why we wanted to meet you here. We were thinking Saltorg could do some tests and look into why this works. Maybe he could find out if there are other ways to make a vampire," said Dienco.

Ruhsarr nodded his head.

"That is interesting. The idea seems to hold water. The dragon's blood has changed us. Our blood must also have some properties that may change humans in the same way. If anyone can work this out it's Saltorg. I need you to do this for us, Saltorg, for our species," said Ruhsarr.

Saltorg look up at him.

"It would be and honour, my Lord," said Saltorg.

"Very good. I want you to begin looking into this straight away. You can have all the resources and humans you need," said Ruhsarr.

"Can Unet and Collu stay here? They are very important now. They are the only two vampires that have been made in this way, that we know about," said Saltorg.

Ruhsarr looked at Dienco who nodded. They both then looked at Saltorg.

"Yes, I presume you will need them, to answer your questions. Maybe guide you with their experiences," said Ruhsarr.

Unet frowned.

"So, I'm just a thing to be passed around? Do I not have a say in this?" she said quite suddenly.

Ruhsarr looked right at her.

"You will do whatever I deem necessary of you. In your case you are a new generation, a newly formed lower tier vampire. As I am the Lord of all vampires you will do as I command," said Ruhsarr.

As she looked at him an awe fell over her. She fell to her knees and bowed her head.

"Yes, my Lord," she said.

The same thing then happened to Collu.

"My Lord," he said.

Ruhsarr ground his teeth together. They made a sound similar to rocks grinding over each other in the sea. He huffed a snort of exasperation from his nose.

"That is more like it," he said.

Chapter 38.

After Ruhsarr, Dienco and Khllet had left, Saltorg guided the two new vampires to the room beyond the table where five elder humans had once sat as a council. He was using this as his own home now. inside this room there was a firepit complete with hotplates and utensils. The floor surrounding the fire was covered with animal skins and blankets.

"Please, sit down. I have many questions," said Saltorg.

Unet looked at Collu who raised his eyebrows, then they both sat down on the floor.

"What do you want to know?" said Unet.

Saltorg smiled.

"You are newly made vampires. Have you tested your abilities?"

"Abilities?" said Unet and Collu at the same time.

"Yes. Your speed, your strength. Are you affected by sunlight in the same way as Khllet of can you resists it light for a while like Dienco and me?" said Saltorg.

Unet and Collu looked at each other and then back at him.

"We have not been told about abilities. Dienco and Khllet have only told us that we need to drink blood to survive," said Collu.

Saltorg pressed his lips together as he thought for a moment.

"That does sound like Dienco. Between you and me, he is a little untrusting. He only tells people what he deems them worthy of knowing. He probably hasn't told you about your abilities as he doesn't want you running off into the night. I understand you were meant to only be drank from," said Saltorg.

Unet nodded her head and tears welled in her eyes.

“Yes. If I hadn’t bit Khllet we would both be dead now. I never asked to be this. I didn’t want to be a vampire. I have two children. Their father died a year ago. I don’t know where they are now,” she said.

The tears in her eyes threatened to fall. She blinked and they rolled down her face. Saltorg took her hands in his.

“I never asked to be a vampire either. The way I look at this is as an opportunity to do things I never could has as a human. I have the speed, power, and strength to build things I couldn’t have done before. If you can take some hope from that it will give you heart to continue as you are. You could go and find you children soon,” he said.

“Now?” she said with a hopeful smile.

“I will arrange for you to go and look for your children tomorrow night. First though I would appreciate if you could help me with some tests,” Saltorg said with a smile.

Unet looked into his ice cold eyes and fought to keep the hopeful expression on her face.

“The first thing I want to do is test your strength. The stones out there are the heaviest thing I can lift. Come with me,” said Saltorg as he got to his feet.

The two new vampires followed him. He walked over to one of the stones, bent down and laid his arms over it and gripped the edge with his fingers. He then pushed then pull it to rock the stone and pulled it onto its side. From that position he held it under his arm and lifted it off the ground. Unet and Collu’s jaws hung slack at the immense strength he displayed. Saltorg looked at them both and smiled.

“This is nothing, Lord Ruhsarr can pick up and throw stones this size,” he said.

Unet and Collu raised their eyebrows. Saltorg then gently set the stone back down on the ground and stepped away.

"You try," he said, gesturing with an outstretched arm.

Unet stepped forwards reached her arm across the stone slab in the same way Saltorg had done. To her own amazement she managed to lift it from the ground.

"How...how is this possible?" she said the shock clear in her voice.

"The vampirism amplifies all of our physical abilities far beyond those of any human. Can you lift it any higher?" said Saltorg.

She worked to raise it and got it up onto her shoulder. She tried to raise it high and found she could get it now higher.

"That's it. I can't quite get it any higher," she said.

"Good. That's great. Now put it down," said Saltorg.

It slipped a little through her hands, but she caught it. She placed the end of the stone on the ground then carefully placed it back down. Collu stepped forwards with a smug smile on his face. He lifted the stone slab up to his waist. He attempted to bring it up further. It was a struggle but after a moment he had it perched on his shoulder. He held it there for a second before he began to fall backwards. The end of the stone hit the ground and Saltorg and Unet caught the stone before the weight of it crushed him.

"What was the purpose of this?" said Unet.

"The vampirism realigns the structures of the human body when we are turned. The muscles are refined and can fire faster and contract to a much denser level against bones that are many times stronger than they were before. It allows us to move

at a vaster rate and lift for more weight than any human could," said Saltorg.
Unet looked at him with a confused expression.
"We are faster and stronger as vampires," he said.
She raised her eyebrows and nodded her head. Saltorg just smiled at her knowing she didn't understand what he had just said.
"Ok. Let's go for a run," he said.
He set off running and went out the door. By the time the two new vampires reached it he was nowhere to be seen. The cacophony of the towns people working and talking carried up the hill to Saltorg's building. A noise cut through it all. The voice of Saltorg.
"Hey! Hello! Over here," he said.
They looked around scanning the town. Unet stopped and nudged Collu's shoulder. A smile played across her face.
"Over there," she said and pointed her index finger out over the town.
Collu followed in the direction she indicated and there is the distance standing on the wall was the silhouette of Saltorg, waving his hands.
"Hello. Stay there," he said.
A few seconds later he blurred to a standstill infront of them.
"Please, tell us, how do you do that," said Unet.
Saltorg smiled, exposing his long, serrated teeth.
"You just run, but you have to push through the limitations your human mind has put in place. You need to push through and release the vampire. Be who you are now, not the human you were," said Saltorg.
Unet and Collu smiled at him.
"Follow me. We'll take it slow at first then speed up," he said.
He started out in a steady jog no faster that a human.

"Let's go a little faster," he said.
They all sped up to a human run. As they passed through the town gates he sped up again to a sprint. He went faster still and they kept up. Then even faster until he began to outpace them. Unet and Collu pushed harder and caught up. He pushed for more speed and Unet kept up, but they started to leave Collu behind. He pushed but no matter how hard he tried they were too fast for him. Saltorg looked at Unet and sped up even more. She tried but could match him for speed. He pointed to the right, Unet looked in the direction and saw that the land was whipping past them. The rolling hills and mountains in the distance seemed to be shifting past her. She looks ahead of her and Saltorg left her behind as he shrank off into the distance. Suddenly he was growing and not running but hurtling towards her. She understood then that he was stood still, and it was she who was running towards him. She stopped in front of him panting to catch her breath. Moments later Collu was standing next to them. Both were panting.

"Good, well done. We have come far," said Saltorg.

"That didn't seem like that far," said Collu.

"Look around you. Where are we?" said Saltorg.
Collu turned and looked around them. He had a confused expression on his face for a moment. Then he smiled.

"I know this place. We're not far from Borsh farm...but Aslakvaas is a day's walk away from here," he said.

Saltorg smiled at him.

"Oh shit. We have run a day's walk in a few moments," said Collu.

"Yes, we have. This is how fast you are now. You can run that fast at any time you like. Just know that you can. Let go of your restrictive human mind," said Saltorg.

"You were going faster than both of us just then. Why is that?" said Unet.

"I don't know. Maybe it's just due to individual ability. I suspect that maybe the vampirism degrades with each generation. So I'm stronger and faster than the two of you because I am the same generation as Dienco. But you, Unet, are faster than Collu because you are the generation above. It is only a suspicion. We will have to do more research into this. Right now though, let's get back to Aslakvaas," said Saltorg.

A short while later they were all back in Saltorg's home.

"I need to turn more humans into vampires. I would appreciate it you help me make more 5th and 6th generations. Then they can begin to make 7th and 8th generations too," said Saltorg.

"So you want us to just go round biting people?" said Unet.

"No. I have 3rd generation vampires who can help you. I also have humans who I've promised to turn. They will be willing to be bitten," said Saltorg.

"I understand the generational things you talked about. How the vampirism may weaken as it spreads, but why will you need so many," said Unet. Saltorg smiled.

"I will need a larger group of vampires to draw information from. The more vampires I have the larger amount of information I can gather," said Saltorg.

Unet raised her eyebrows and nodded again. Saltorg smiled a little devious smile.

"Now, please relax. I have some things I must attend to," he said. He moved and an instant later was gone.

Unet side eyed Collu, then looked directly at him.

"Do you trust him?" she said.

Collu shrugged.

"I don't know. I never met a vampire I trusted before. I suppose things are different now that we're vampires too," he said.

"I still don't trust him. Why does he want us to make so many more vampires?" she said.

Collu shrugged.

"I think he needs vampires to do experiments on. Vampires who won't be missed. He's not offering up himself or his family of blood or whatever he called them," she said.

Collu's eyes widened.

"You think he means to kill us even though we are vampires?" he said.

"Maybe not kill us, but we are definitely in harms way, and I suspect whatever he has in mind will be painful too," she said.

Chapter 39.

A few weeks passed and Unet and Collu had worked out the neck and wrists were the best areas to bite to quickly and easily access blood. To turn a human into a vampire only a small amount of blood would need to be exchanged. Subsequently they had twenty generations of vampires. Forty eight vampires in all from their initial two. Saltorg had become insistent that they make more to the point that he would become nasty if he thought they were taking too long. He grew angry if any these new vampires refused to do his bidding.

This day was different. There was a hopeful glint in his eye. He had them all gathered together in a circle around him in the old temple.

"Lord Ruhsarr became the first vampire after he was attacked by a dragon and its blood got into his wounds. He later turned into the magnificent being he is now and after a ferocious battle he mortally wounded the dragon. Before it could decay and return to the earth he collected its blood. He later fed that blood to me and the other members of the children of the blood. It improved us, perfected us. You have been made into vampires by drinking human blood. Up to now everyone has only drunk human blood. What would happen if a vampire were to drink vampire blood? Would it improve us the same way the dragon's blood has done to me and my brethren? The only way to find out is to try. Tul, Hani. Please step forward," he said.

The two newest vampires approached him and stood side by side in front of him.

"Now. Tul, I want you to bite Hani," he said.

Hani was short with a stocky build. Tul was taller and slim. He stepped towards Hani and placed his hands on his shoulders. He opened his mouth and leaned in towards Hani's neck. For moment he hesitated.

"Go on, what are you waiting for? An invite?" barked Saltorg.

Tul did as he was told and bit into Hani's neck. He only meant to drink a little, but his jaw clenched and tore a chunk of flesh from Hani. He clamped his mouth over the wound and began to gulp down the blood that flowed freely. Hani push the palm of his hand against Tul's forehead and tried to push him away to no avail. Then he punched his fists up into Tul's chest, but he just held on tighter.

"Get him off me," Hani shouted.

Half a dozen vampires ran to help but no matter how they fought Tul wouldn't let go. Hani's flesh began to shrivel as all the blood was drained from him. Then Tul released his grip and roared so loud it reverberated through the building. Hani threw a weak punched into his face. Tul placed his hands on both sides of Hani's head, and with no visible effort, tore it from his body. The vampires who were trying to help stood back in shock. The head and the body then burned up and shot out burning embers. The surrounding vampires screamed and some tried to flee. Moments later Hani was nothing but ashes.

"Stand strong people!" called Saltorg above the screams.

Tul leapt on the closest vampire and tore into her. His strength was immense and when she tried to slap him away he took hold of her arm and pulled it from her body like a wing from a fly. It burned up and turned to ash as he cast it aside. Moments later the vampire was little more than a husk. He discarded her without a thought. Then leapt on to the back of another and made short work of draining him. He locked eyes with Saltorg. As this raging beast of a vampire ran at him Saltorg reached out and took Unet by the hair. He then swung her into Tul's path. With terrifying strength he pulled Unet to pieces and continued on his way to Saltorg.

"Protect me," he cried.

A few of the vampires did step in front of Tul but the power coursing through him made him seemingly unstoppable. He tore through them like a tiger through a flock of chickens. Saltorg realised that he would have to stand and fight. He stepped in and racked his clawed hand through Tul's throat, but the flesh repaired itself instantly. He ran from this monster then turned and ran directly at him. They collided and Tul was thrown all he way to the far wall of the building. Saltorg watched in horror a This thing stood back up unscathed. He took one step forwards then threw his head back and roared. A huge blue flame shot up from his mouth and quickly engulfed his entire body. He thrashed and writhed, swinging his arms about him. Through the roar of the flames his screams could be heard. He was in agony. A few seconds later he burnt completely to ash. The other vampires were all still running and hiding.

"Woah. People come back. It's over," said Saltorg.

"What the fuck happened to him?" said someone. Everyone stood and stared shock and dumbfounded by the pile of ash and still smouldering bones.

"You!" barked Collu pointing at Saltorg. "Did you know that was going to happen?"

"No, I honestly had no idea," said Saltorg.

Tears welled in Collu's eyes.

"You didn't know this would happen, or you didn't know what would happen at all?" hissed Collu.

"I'm running on impulse here. We are standing on the edge of discovery. Nothing is certain," said Saltorg.

"Unet is dead! Tul, Hani, Trove, and Ooni are dead!" snarled Collu.

"This is the way of the world. People die constantly. You better get used to it."

Saltorg was cut off as Collu flew at him and grabbed him by the throat roaring as he did. A look of shock spread across Saltorg's face but was quickly replaced by one of anger. He knocked Collu's hands away and clamped his hands on either side of his head. Collu's roar became a scream of pain as the bones of his skull collapsed. With a final crunch and a spurt of blood Collu's eyes burst from their sockets and the top of his head split like a broken watermelon. With a twist of his hands Saltorg tore the remains of the vampire's head away and threw it too the ground where it burnt to ash along with the body. He looked around him and all the vampires. All their attention wad on him now. Some looked shocked, while others looked scared. Some were even crying.

"Some of you are forgetting your place. Beside Lord Ruhsarr, I am your master! You attack me, you might as well be attacking lord Ruhsarr. Things are going to change around here. I have let you get away with treating me like one of you for far too long. I didn't want it to come to this but from now on I will not hesitate to kill anyone of you who steps out of line of disobeys me!" he roared.

The vampires nodded.

"My Lord?" whispered one of them.

"Silence. We have learned today that we cannot drink the blood of other vampires. Now, clean up this mess!" he said.

The vampires nodded silently and got to work cleaning up the ashes while he strode away.

Chapter 40.

News of Saltorg's discoveries, and his barbarity, travelled fast through the vampire communities. As a result groups of vampires began to faction off from the main communities that surrounded Ruhsarr and the Children of the Blood. They spread out across the lands. The further these factions became generationally from Lord Ruhsarr the more susceptible they became to the effects of silver, sunlight and other pure natural elements.

Saltorg continued to work on his experiments into vampiric adaption. He tried creating poultices and elixirs to allow them to walk in the sun but nothing he tried ever worked. The effect of vampires drinking vampire blood, that soon became referred to as 'Blood Fire', was adopted as a punishment for those he and the collective vampire hierarchy saw as traitors and criminals. As did 'Dawnlighting', the act of tying a vampire to a stake and leaving them to the ravages of the first rays of the morning sun. Subsequently the number of vampires who stepped out of line dropped dramatically.

Chapter 41.

A decade after Ruhsarr had killed Azangor, vampires began to be able to reproduce in the usual manner again. Now, over one thousand years after Ruhsarr and his army had sacked the town, half the vampires that called Fallohade their home had never been human. This place that had once been a dwelling of only a dozen houses had grown steadily and now contained more than one thousand buildings.

Many more towers had been built in Fallohade as the town spread out over the years. However, the original tower still stood in its centre. The walls of the town had been built thicker and higher than those that stood before. As a result any bands of humans who had tried to attack the town stood little chance of getting beyond them. But even a few hundred humans was no match for the hundreds of vampires who called Fallohade town their home. Any human attackers who weren't killed or turned were stored as food. Some were used as practice for young vampires to hone their killing techniques.

Chapter 42.

It was a cold winters evening, and snow had fallen over the land a few days before. Most of it had melted now but some still remained in patches. The wind whistled around the central tower. It found its way inside and bothered the flames of the fire that the occupants warmed themselves beside. In the top floor room, Ruhsarr sat feeding on a man he had captured that evening. In the darkness that surrounded the tower, guard vampires patrolled the walls. The town was not lit by flaming torches as human towns were. The moon and the stars provided more than enough light for their vampire eyes to see perfectly. Despite the enhanced levels of vision their eyes provided none of them notice a shadow that ran silently along the top of the wall. By the time one of the guards noticed the shadow had already pushed a blade through his heart and turned him to dust. He never even got to make a sound. It quickly dispatched another two vampires then leapt from the wall into the town. It hit the damp ground and rolled without making a sound. As it moved between the huts and buildings it assassinated any vampire that crossed its path. None of whom got out more than a gasp or wheeze before any of them were aware of its presence. It jumped up onto the roof of a building and leapt from one to the other in a smooth and elegant almost weightless movement. A guard at the top of one of the towers finally saw the intruder. She roared out an alarm call in the form of a long, high pitched and extremely loud wail. The shadow threw a small blade that split the guard's heart in two, but it was already too late. The whole town was alerted. The shadow moved faster now, it flitted from building to building, but the vampire guards were on its tail. It launched itself from a rooftop and landed on the wall of the tower from where the alarm call had been raised. It scaled the wall at speed, but a group of vampires were in close pursuit. It reached the top and ran to the opposite edge. The pursuing vampires reach the top close behind it. The shadow turned and threw tiny ceramic boxes at their feet, which broke against the hard, wooden roof. Each emitted a silvery smoke. As it surrounded them it ate their flesh causing them to writhe in agony. They tried to scream but the smoke ate through their throats and lungs. Moments later they were little more than ash and bones. The smoke cleared and more vampires reached the roof just in time to see the shadowy figure take a swan dive off the edge of the tower. One dived off after it, but the others hesitated. The shadow hurtled towards the ground then landed in a crouched position; one foot, one knee and one hand. The other arm outstretched held a long black pole weapon, a Naginata. It had a crescent moon shape blade on one end, and a long, slim blade on the other. A crowd a vampires swarmed to surround this intruder but kept a distance of a few feet. They all jumped back even further as a screaming vampire slammed into the ground and became a mess of shattered bones and torn flesh. The shadow straightened up and held the Naginata by its side. Now that it stood still the crowd could see the figure was 6 feet 5 inches, female, and covered from head to toe in a close-fitting black fabric. There was an eerie stillness about the intruder. It looked at the crowd, its eyes focusing on one among them and then moving to another. The crowd looked right back at it. They snarled and shifted around waiting for this creature to make a move. Likewise, she patiently waited for one among them to be brave, or foolish, enough to make the first move. Eventually, the stillness was broken when a tall vampire roared and ran out from the crowd swinging an axe over his head. The shadow quickly stepped forwards, simultaneously she thrust the crescent blade out and through his neck. His head fell from his body to the ground. As it landed it shattered into a pile of ash. The crowd of vampires stared in shock for a moment. A few of them stepped back a few paces. Then one among them hissed. The rest began to follow suit and soon they all hissed and snarled. They closed in to attack her, but she spun the naginata over her head and then swung the blades through them. Heads were liberated from necks, and torsos were sliced apart. Despite this, the vampires continued to charge. She flipped and vaulted through them swinging and jabbing the pole into their rage fuelled bodies as she went. Limbs were cleaved from their owners and turned to ash as they travelled through the air. She made light work of this crowd, and their numbers dwindled before they realised they were not going to win this fight.

Guards were trying to get near her but in the confusion she had manipulated the remaining crowd into moving down through the streets towards the central tower. She threw a handful of the little boxes into the crowd. The smoke did its work burning away their flesh to the bones. Most of them fell to the ground writhing as they disintegrated. A few managed to slip away while suffering choking coughs. She took this chance to run towards the door of the tower.

As she got closer it began to open. She leapt at it and landed with all her weight directly in the centre. The hinges were destroyed, and the door was launched into the room. The unlucky guard behind it became trapped beneath. He was crush and ground to dust. It came to a halt on the opposite side of the room with her stood upon it. She deftly swung the long blade of her Naginata up between the legs of a guard as he strode towards her, splitting him in two. She now had the full attention of the entire room. With an otherworldly speed and grace she navigated her way across the room moving amongst the guards. She swung and slashed her weapon as she passed it from one hand to the other. This sent lumps of burning vampire cascading in all directions. She began to climb the stairs leaving a trail if ash and destruction in her wake.

The wooden staircase wound its way around the inner wall of the tower leading to the higher floors, and eventually to the top floor. More guards gave chase, so with a quick twist on the handle, the Naginata split into two shorter close combat weapons. With these she dismembered and killed any vampire who tried to attack her as she passed them in the confined space of the staircase.

Eventually, she reached the top floor covered in ash and dust. A huge and locked solid oak door blocked her path. She ran and dropkicked it, only to fall to the floor when it refused to budge. A group of guards came running up the stairs towards her. She jumped to her feet and sliced the first one in half, then decapitated the next. She turned, kicked the door with all her might then spun, split another guard in half and took off another's legs. She turned and kicked the door again. This time it cracked but stayed together. More guards came running up the stairs. She attacked them too, cutting off heads, arms and legs. She was stood, breathing heavily and drenched in ash and blood. The door swung open. Not from her efforts, but because it was opened from the other side. Beyond it stood a huge silhouette that filled the doorway.

"I assume you're looking for me?" boomed the

voice of Ruhsarr.
His appearance had changed over the past one thousand years. He stood at eight feet tall, his scales were twice as thick, and his muscle mass had doubled. A row of horns ran from over both his earholes and met at the crown of his skull.

She launched straight into an attack and ran at him with both blades ready, but he quickly stepped aside. A quick turn and she threw her whole weight at him, but he easily swept her away with a strong block from his forearm. She hit the floor, slid and rolled, then jumped back to her feet. Again, she came at him, but with a swift front kick he sent her stumbling back into a wall. She pushed herself from its surface and leapt at him while swinging her blades. He caught her by the head, spun and let her go. As he did she slashed his arm open, before she collided with a table. She tried to flip over it in a controlled crouched position, but it shattered. Quick reactions helped her land on her feet. Ruhsarr raised his arm and smiled at her as the deep wound healed instantly. She threw the long blade at him while he gloated. The pain as it lodged itself between his ribs wiped the smile from his face. He took hold of the handle, and no longer concentrating on her, he didn't see her run at him. He pulled out the blade and dropped it just as she landed on his right shoulder. Repeatedly she thrust a short thin blade into his face just below his left eye. He grabbed her leg, pulled her away from him and held her up off the ground in front of him. A snarl rose in his throat, but in a show of defiance she slashed at him with the blade. The initial flames of anger sparked to life inside him. He grabbed her arm and snapped her elbow. She screamed in agony just before he slammed her head into the floor. Bones broke apart under his hand and her screams stopped. He straightened up and turned around. He was about to walk away and call for guards to remove her body when something hit him in the back. He turned around to see her getting to her feet as her skull slid back into shape. She opened her mouth wide and moved her head from side to side. Her bones clicked and her head was back to normal. She then raised her left arm in front of her and it dangled limp at the elbow. With a quick flick of the limb, and an audible crunch, the joint realigned itself. The surrounding muscles and tendons moved back into place under the skin and black material. She pointed a finger of the same hand at him.

"I came here to kill you, yet you dishonour me. You would turn your back on a fight before it is over? I was expecting more from the 'Great' Ruhsarr Miehyelzah. You will pay for your insolence!" she said

He reacted exactly the way she expected him to, with overblown arrogant rage.

"You attack me in my home, them claim that I am insolent? I will take your head for a trophy!" he roared.

A flash of movement from her arm sent a handful of the ceramic boxes smashing at his feet. They broke open and the smoke surrounded him. A cough came from the cloud of smoke, then a roar bellowed from his lungs as he strode out from it. The shadow stood her ground as he charged at her. When he was right infront of her, she jumped up just over him, kicked both feet down into the top of his head and summersaulted over him. His chin took the brunt of his weight as he crashed down to the floor. She landed and turned to look at this giant beast. He lay still for a moment but then hauled himself up. A drop kicked to the back with both her feet launched him forwards. He would have landed on his face again but with a quick tuck and a roll he stood up. Then spun around and saw her come at him again. With a powerful uppercut he sent her sprawling across the room. Her body hit the floor with a thud, but instantly she flipped herself up onto her feet. Just in time to see him running at her with his head down. He threw out his wings and flew at her like a winged battering ram. His shoulder connected with her chest, smashed her ribs and sent her crashing to the floor. She lay sprawled and gasping for breath. While he landed with ease, pulled in his wings, and folded them down. He turned, walked over and reached down for her. She tried to avoid his hand, but he grabbed her by the ankles and swung her in a circle above his head then let go. Furniture and pottery splintered and shattered around her before she hit the wall. The pain of her skull and shoulder shattering was horrendous. She felt the rage build up and threaten to break out of her.

"Control. Stay in control," she whispered to herself, and took a few deep breaths.

He strode towards her and let out a victorious roar. As she struggled to her feet the pain surged through her head and shoulder. She noticed him charge at her and despite the pain from her broken bones she had no choice but to jump over him. He smashed his fists into the wall. Landing heavily she willed herself to run across the room. She rolled her shoulder as she moved, hearing it crack back into place. She stopped as far from him as she could be, allowing time for her skull realign itself and heal. Ruhsarr turned and shook his hands, then immediately he ran, spread out his wings and flew at her again. Through clenched teeth she hiss at him, then ran and pulled a Kitana blade from the scabbard strapped to her back. She leapt over him and with a lightning quick movement of the blade she sliced off both his wings. The floor shook as he fell face-first into it. Closely followed by the mass of his body as he crashed down and slid for several feet. His wings landed on either side of the woman as she landed gracefully. They twitched with muscles spasmed, then the flesh hardened, and they burned to ash. The figure quickly ran back to her enemy and climbed on his back. Blood poured from the stumps where his wings had been, but they were already beginning to heal. She stabbed him between his shoulder blades, and he let out a roar of pain. She plunged the blade into him several more times. Thrashing his arms, he bucked like a horse in an attempt to throw her off, but she wrapped her legs around his waist and held on. He made to stand up, so she quickly climbed to his shoulders and jumped straight up. She rotated in the air and as her feet touched the ceiling she pushed off with all her might. This launched her back at the monster with her blade pointed right at him. There was nothing he could do. He had no time to react. The blade pierced his face through his left nostril and stuck out of the back of his head. He began to fall. As he did, she yanked the blade out to the left and sliced that side of his head wide open. He hit the floor and choked as blood poured down his throat from the wound. Landing on his chest she drew the blade over her head and plunged it deep into him, right up to the hilt. The end of the blade exited through his back and wedged itself into the floor. As she tried to pull it out she found that it was wedged into the stone below him. His hand enveloped her head as he grabbed her threw her aside. He placed his hands on the floor on either side of him and pushed against it. The blade resisted for a moment but then came free. He got to his feet, seized the handle and pulled the Kitana from his chest. He stood and held his head for a moment as the wounds healed. The woman had no intention of giving him any reprieve. She ran up and kicked him in his abdomen. He stumbled back a few paces but remained upright. She tried again but he slapped her aside. The next time she came at him he swung the blade at her head. She managed to avoid it, but the tip snagged the material covering her face. When she turned her head to look at him again, he saw her green reptilian eye, and purple scaled skin. A long, lock of blonde hair fell free from the gap in the material.

"Who are you? Who sent you here?" he said.

"You should know the answers to your questions. after all, you did create me!" she said.

She launched herself at him, but he caught her and slammed her down into the floor. Punches to his forearm did nothing. His grip was too strong, and she couldn't move him. The rage came again, strong and chaotic. This time she gave herself over to it. The bones of her face shifted and realign themselves into a snout. She opened her jaws wide, and a flicker of light danced at the back of her throat.

"What are you doing?" said Ruhsarr.

She drew in a deep breath. The rage burst from her mouth as a long, loud roar and a huge ball of fire. The flames blasted into his face and chest, white-hot and wicked. They died down as her breath and the roar ran out. Above her she saw his face somehow remained undamaged. His mouth was curled in an arrogant smile.

"That was impressive. It's a cruel twist of irony though that one of your most destructive abilities is entirely useless against me," he said.

A slow laugh began in his throat. Her face twisted into a grimace, and she pulled a short dagger from her belt and slashed it across the inside of his elbow splitting flesh, muscles, and tendons. He pulled his arm away and growled at her. Hissing deep and low in her throat, she jumped on him. Quickly wrapping her legs around his neck. She dug her fingers into his eye sockets and pulled in opposite directions. The bones of his skull began to shift. Jelly and blood from his eyes spilt over her hands. Unable to see he took hold of her and pulled but she refused to let go. He put his head down then ran as hard as he could and slammed them both into a wall. Chunks of stone flew in all directions and dust filled the air. They both crumpled to the floor and lay there dazed and disorientated. After a few moments he got up to his knees as she was coming round. He stood up, shook his head then squeezed his eyelids shut. When he opened them his eyeballs were fully reformed. She was just getting to her feet when he picked her up by the waist and slammed her into the wall. The room shook. He pulled her back then this time threw her against the damaged wall. Bricks were knocked loose and the whole wall shifted. The room began to shake as more bricks fell down into the streets below. The ceiling began to cave in and the floor below them heaved and rumbled. The room gave one last stomach lurching tilt and fell along with the side of the tower, taking them with it, down into the street below. Tons of stone and wood fell around them. Any vampires who were unfortunate enough to be in the way were crushed. The whole town shook with the impact, Ruhsarr and the woman were lost in the debris.

As the dust cleared a pile of stones moved and were pushed aside. The woman stood up, she placed her hand on her side and pushed her ribs back into place then took a breath. She began to walk away from the remains of the tower when a large pile of stone moved. She reached for one of her weapons but found that she had lost them all.

Ruhsarr heaved a slab up above his head. She ran at the weakened tower wall and threw herself at it with all her strength. The was a deep rumble as more of the stones shifted then fell and crushed Ruhsarr's torso beneath the slap he was holding. She walked towards him, but his arms were still free and still dangerous. He struggled against the weight of stone that held him and was working himself free. She backed away.

"It is now you who is walking away from the fight. Without your weapons you are no match for me," he said.

"I am making a calculated retreat. You are a great warrior, I admit, I underestimated your strength and abilities," she said.

"Admit defeat and I will spare your life."

"I will do no such thing, but mark my words, this is not over. We will meet again and next time I will kill you," she said.

"Next time we meet I'm going to tear out your heart and eat it infront of you!" he said.

She gave him a stern stare.

"I once said that I would take on the world with you if I had to. That is no longer true. You have become the very thing you swore to destroy. I will find a way of ridding the world of you. I'm going to make sure the dragon's curse comes into fruition," she said.

Deep inside his mind in a place that he thought had been erased he recognised those words. His jaw swung loose and for a moment he was speechless.

"You. I thought I killed you," he said.

She didn't answer. She just smiled and winked before she turned and ran. Ruhsarr managed to heave the tonnes of rubble off himself and got to his feet. A group of guards lead by Helden, Dienco's son, ran over to him and tried to help, but he pushed them away.

"Ah, finally. How kind of you to turn up," said Ruhsarr wryly.

"Which way did she go, my Lord? We-we could still follow her," said Helden.

"No, that would be a bad idea. She has killed enough of you already. Besides, if I couldn't beat her what chance do you have," said Ruhsarr.

"Yes Master. I apologise profusely, my Lord," said Helden.

Ruhsarr looked him straight in the eye.

"How did she get in here!? Into the town and all the way to the top of my tower! There were over one thousand vampires within these walls and one warrior got all the way to me. What good are you all as guards if you as a collective can't stop one trespasser?" said Ruhsarr.

"I am sorry and take full responsibility for this deplorable mistake. Please accept my apology, my Lord," said Helden. He bowed his head and knelt before Ruhsarr.

"This display was an embarrassment to you all, and most of all me. As a result, I'm stripping you, Helden, of your rank. The fact that your father is Captain Dienco is the only reason I allow you to live," said Ruhsarr.

Helden bowed his head. He could feel the eyes of the other guards on him. He could feel their contempt.

"Yes, my Lord. Thank you, my Lord," he said.

Ruhsarr pointed at the guard stood to the right of him.

"What is your name?" he said.

"Yolsin, my Lord," she said.

"You are my new Captain," he said.

"Thank you for this great opportunity, my Lord," said the Guard.

"You're welcome. Prove your worthy or I *will* find another who is."

"Yes, my Lord. Understood my Lord," said Yolsin as she stood to attention.

"Now leave me, all of you, before I unleash my true anger on you."

"Yes, my Lord," said all the guards in unison and moved quickly away.

Ruhsarr stood seething. This attack had shown that he was vulnerable. He would have to redeem himself and reaffirm his reputation as Lord of all vampires. There was a viable threat to them now. She was out there, she was dangerous, and she was an efficient vampire killer.

He dug through the rubble and found the vase that had contained the dragon's blood. A large hole had been broken in one side. Only a small amount of the blood he collected remained. It was covered in dust and beginning to congeal. He lifted the vase and poured it into his mouth. It oozed from the vase like syrup. It felt thick and gritty on his tongue, but he didn't care. He needed it. He swallowed and felt the power if it spread over his entire body. Hard bone spines pushed out through the flesh over his spine. More small horns pushed out from the flesh of his skull. His scales grew thicker and harder, and in some areas began to merge together to form plates of armour.

"I know now who you are. I know you will return. When you do, I will be ready!" he said quietly.

Chapter 43 – Epilogue.

Ruhsarr stepped out from the opening of an old flint mine dug deep into the heart of the mountain, Old Man of Coniston. It now served as his mountain hideout. He looked out across the landscape and watched as the sun dipped towards the peaks of the mountains in the Peak District in Northwest England. A smile played across his face. He opened his wings and spread them out to their full span. He gave them a few slow test flaps, then pulled them in. He leapt high into the fridged mountain air, spread his wings again, and flapped them down hard. This action took him high into the atmosphere.

He flew in circles over the city of Lancaster and the surrounding towns for a while, before heading further south. Soon he was circling over the city of Manchester. He was hunting for a certain type of prey this night. In his arrogance he liked to tempt the dragon's curse. He had done this many times before and tonight he thought the results would be no different. He descended over a housing estate. There, he saw her. A young pregnant woman walking towards an alley way. Her mousy brown hair was tussled but the cold December wind. He flew overhead, then turned back and landed behind her.

The end is the beginning is the end…

If you have enjoyed this book and this trilogy please tell your friends, post about it on social media, in your blog, or talk about it on your podcast. Word of mouth is the most valuable resource to us self published authors.
Thank you in advance.

Thoughts from the author.

So, here we are. The end. 15 years' worth of hard work and learning on the job. I started out with not much in the way of writing knowledge. All I knew was that I had stories and I wanted to share them. I didn't realise back then how long this would take to write. I thought it would just be a short story to add to a collection or an anthology or maybe get it published in a magazine. I never envisioned it would take this amount of time or become such an expansive story with such deep lore. I learnt all about grammar, vocabulary, and codex. I have learnt styles, strategies and techniques. I've learnt about publishing, formatting, and cover designing. Don't get me wrong I'm no graphic designer but I have designed all of my book covers to some extent, from cropping stock photos to hand drawing some of the elements in the designs. The process of self publishing has changed since I first started publishing too. It has gotten easier to put your work out into the world. For better and in some case for worse too. I swear to you now, nothing you ever read or see in any my books will ever be AI generated. Social media has changed completely since I started posting too. Back then you could post stuff and everyone on your friends list would see it. Now most people are lucky to get 400 views. Like I could easily put out a post about my writing journey and it would be seen far and wide and now they expect you to pay for a post to be seen 1000 people. They have made it so hard to be a self published author, or an artist. It's been an extremely interesting time. So much has happened in the time that it has taken me to write these books. The hunted aott and We, the Damned included.

Sadly, my grandad died in the year I started writing, and my grandma died before I published The Hunted and other twisted tales. My father-in-law also died almost a year before I could publish this book. I have lost friends to self harm, depression and bipolar disorder. I will always remember them. I myself have suffered heartbreak, anxiety, depression. I was made redundant in 2014 but found more work. Early in 2020 I was diagnosed with a rare genetic change named 17q12 microduplication syndrome. It can affect the development of internal organs and cause a range of mental health disorders. I have been quite lucky that it has only caused me to have depression, anxiety and I suspect ADHD and dyslexia. A little later that year I was furloughed for nearly a year. We all know why. That was and interesting time. I got a lot of work done on this trilogy and We the Damned. I would get up at around 10 am and switch on my computer, have some breakfast and then start working. I got a little glimpse into what it would be like as a working author. Despite all the other hardships of the time I enjoyed the time I had. The five years since have been a little surreal.

On the flip side though, I have met the love of my life, my wife Carrie, we have raised our two kids and got married. I love my kids. I love watching them grow up, seeing the people they are becoming. Marriage and children, when I started writing, were things I had no idea were even on the cards for me. My wife and I bought our house together nearly 11 years ago. It feels like a few years at most. It has been such an enjoyable time in my life. I have also become an uncle three times and it is an honour to be part of my expanding family's lives. I was the best man at my best friend's wedding, which is also just as much an honour to be part of Phil and Karis' lives that they think that much of me. Meeting readers and making friends both physically and digitally. I appreciate you all so much. There are a range of other great and wonderful things that have happened but too many to mention.

So it's more than fair to say it has been a time of ups and downs.

If you are reading this, thank you so much for your support. I appreciate you taking the time to come along with me on the journey. I love and appreciate you.

I loved creating all the characters and the world I have built. It is as important to me as this real world we all inhabit. The lore has been so interesting to build and evolve. To see it shape the characters physically and the affects it has on their abilities.

I have had so much fun in the world of Alex, Andra, Ruhsarr, the S.O.V.E.U. and the Children of the Blood. However, the time has come to move on to other stories. I have already begun working on another book. One completely unrelated to this world of the military, vampires and dragons. It is already shaping up to be less high octane than the Beasts of Immortality trilogy, but to be fair, that isn't hard to do. Obviously it will have a heavy paranormal element, I just want to spread my wings into other areas and tell different long form stories. One day I may return to the blood soaked sandpit of Beasts of Immortality and play around with some of these characters again, but for now I need to give them some well deserved R&R. I am not saying goodbye to them. Just see you later. They will always occupy a space in my mind, as they now occupy a space in yours.

If these books have inspired you to pick up a pen or a pencil, open the word processor app on your computer, or make a piece of art in any form, please, keep going. Believe in yourself, sometimes you have to be your own hype person. Push through the imposter syndrome. If you figure out how to do this tell me how. Believe people when they tell you your work is good. This can be hard to take in sometimes. I know that sounds strange, but it is true. On the flip side of the same coin, be critical of your own work. You will write and create things that need to be changed and removed, no matter how much you love them. It's a necessity of being an artist, it will also help you grow as an artist if you can be self critical, but don't be too critical or you will never finish anything. Most of all, have fun.

Author Bio.

Paul J. Kearns is an author from Bolton, Northwest England. He lives there with his wife and two children. From a young age Paul has had an interest in writing. He is also a fan of all things dark and horrifying. After leaving school he started working as a dental technician and earned a B-Tec National diploma and a UCHE in Dental Technology from the Manchester Metropolitan University. He still works as a Dental Technician today. In his spare time he loves to spend time with his family and friends, writing, watching movies, gaming, and drawing.

Printed in Dunstable, United Kingdom

68465835R10143